I0596113

A Snowflake Wish

USA TODAY BESTSELLING AUTHOR

RENEE HARLESS

RENEE HARLESS

All rights reserved.
ISBN-13: 978-1-7323563-6-8
Copyright ©2019 Renee Harless
This work is one of fiction. Any resemblance of characters to persons, living or deceased, is purely coincidental. Names, places, and characters are figments of the author's imagination. All trademarked items included in this novel have been recognized as so by the author. The author holds exclusive rights to this work. Unauthorized duplication is prohibited.
All rights reserved

Paperback Edition

Image: Shutterstock

Cover design by Porcelain Paper Designs

If there was one thing January Douglas disliked more than spilling coffee on her favorite blouse, it was Christmas. Despite her family's love of the holiday, she was a self-proclaimed Scrooge. The songs, the decorations, and the forced cheer - they were all nails scratching down a chalkboard to her.

When Deckard Spruce barged into her life with his Christmas enthusiasm and a smirk that made January weak in the knees, she'd had enough.

One wish on a snowflake was all it took to change everything, but as soon as the damage was done, she knew her hate for the holidays had gone too far.

Could Deckard help her realize that she might not hate Christmas after all?

Maybe one more wish would make everything right.

RENEE HARLESS

Chapter One

usic filtered into the bedroom from the small rectangular box January kept on her nightstand. She was fond of the old alarm clock that her parents had given her when she was in middle school, always preferring it to the alarm on her mobile phone. But the dreadful song playing through the small speaker only intensified January's desire to grab the box and throw it against the wall.

As the chorus from "I'll be Home for Christmas" continued to fill the room with its melodic verse, January grabbed the closest pillow and chucked it against the box from Hell. When that didn't diminish the sound, she slammed the pillow over her head in hopes of drowning out the remainder of the noise still blaring between her ears.

Just as sleep tiptoed January back into unconsciousness, the phone sitting adjacent to the alarm clock began to play a song meant to torture January even further. She couldn't help but wonder who was out to get her today.

Her hand jutted out, blindly reaching for the device, but her sleep-filled limbs knocked the phone from the nightstand. A groan escaped from January's puckered lips at the loud sound of a clatter against the hardwood floor. Of course, her luck would have her lifeline shattering against the hard surface instead of the soft cushioned rug beneath her bed.

The music continued to play as she reached over the bed. Her eyelids remained squeezed tightly together, trying to fight off the morning.

Without a glimpse at the screen she knew was now cracked, January brought the phone to her ear.

"I hate you so much right now," January mumbled into the receiver.

"Good morning, Sunshine!"

Ignoring her co-worker's chipper attitude, January rolled over in her bed, finally prying her tired eyes open, their dryness making it more difficult than usual.

"Why did you change my ringtone again?"

"Because if anyone could use the Christmas spirit, it's you."

January moved her body languidly as she sat up in bed and turned on the speaker setting for her phone as she spoke with Samantha. Taking a deep breath, January filled her lungs with fresh air at the same time she stretched her arms above her head.

"I thought I told you to stop messing with my phone yesterday."

A disappointed voice sounded on the other end of the call. "Oh, I figured you just didn't like that song."

"Samantha," January chastised, "I haven't liked a single Christmas song for the last two and a half decades."

Silence filled the room as she finished her stretch.

"Samantha?" she prompted.

"I'm sorry. I didn't mean anything by it," her friend replied solemnly.

"I know, and it's okay. Anyway, why the early call?"

"Oh, yes," Samantha's excited voice filled the room again. "I pulled the research you requested on the baking contest and how Ms. Smith is being accused of copying Mr. Daugherty's recipe. And I also got you an interview with the head of the Christmas Festival."

January tossed her legs casually over the side of the bed and stood, the image of her pajama-clad body ignored in the mirror.

"Why do I always get these assignments?"

"Because you're the best reporter in Lifestyles and everyone knows it."

For the first time this morning, a smile graced January's lips. "Thanks. I'll see you soon."

Ending the phone call, January shuffled to the adjacent bathroom, doing her best to ignore the twinkle of tinsel that glistened on her Christmas tree in the corner of her living room - the tree her mother had set up without her knowledge three days ago. But no matter how hard she tried, the soft light coming from the window made the shiny metal hard to ignore.

Her shuffles quickly turned to stomps as she marched into the bathroom and slammed the door shut.

"Ten days. Just ten more days," she mumbled as she ripped off her pajamas and stepped into the shower, twisting the knobs to adjust the water temperature. January was always one of the few that loved the initial chill of the water as it pelted her skin; it's what woke her up every morning. Caffeine had nothing on cold water.

Tugging on a deep-purple sweater and a pair of brown slacks, January prepared herself for work. Just a quick blow-dry of her hair and a few last touches of makeup had her ready with enough time to snag a bagel and hot chocolate at the bakery in town.

January stepped toward her front door, grabbed her keys, purse, and jacket, then closed the door behind her as she walked out to the crisp morning. Dark, gloomy clouds loomed low in the sky, and January knew snow was in the forecast for Pineville, Ohio.

As much as she despised Christmas, January had quite the fondness for winter in general. She loved the snow, the barren landscapes waiting for their regrowth in the spring, the silence when darkness fell on their town and the stars offered the only light. Winter always seemed magical to her.

"Good morning, Samantha," January greeted as she walked into her office with a paper bag in one hand and two large cups of steaming hot chocolate in a carrier in the other.

The petite woman's feet clicked at a quickened pace on the laminate flooring of the office as she rushed toward January. "Is that what I think it is?" the woman whispered in amazement as she took in the loot January carried.

"If you're thinking two cinnamon and sugar bagels and hot cocoa, then you'd be wrong," January joked, doing her best not to laugh at the forlorn expression growing on Samantha's face. January clarified, unable to hold out any longer, "It's two cinnamon and sugar bagels, hot chocolate, and a handful of peppermint drop cookies."

January had never seen someone orgasm from the thought of food, but she was fairly certain she had just witnessed it with her co-worker. Samantha had a sweet tooth unlike anyone she had ever met, and as the woman's cheeks flushed and her breathing became erratic, January was sure she had just observed it happening in the flesh.

As her friend reached out to grab the paper cups, she asked, "Does this mean you're no longer mad at me?"

January answered, with an upward tilt of the corners of her lips, "Maybe. You know I can't ever stay mad at you."

Samantha followed January into her office space, and they set the cups and food on the small table in the corner.

"Now, let's eat some breakfast while you tell me all about the baking allegations and the research you found."

The two friends and co-workers sat with their heads together at the table, switching between taking small bites of their favorite local bagel and taking notes for the article. Ms. Smith claimed that her recipe had been handed down to her from her great grandmother and she had it memorized, whereas Mr. Daugherty said that he had proof of her taking a picture of his recipe card for his award-winning butter pecan cookies when he stupidly left it out during one of the competitions.

Three years ago, the two competed against each other, both making butter pecan cookies. It was Ms. Smith's first year but Mr. Daughtery's tenth. The competition came in at a tie.

January poured over her notes as she finished off her cup of hot chocolate, and Samantha left to take a call in her cubicle across from the office. She couldn't help but wonder why this was such an interesting piece to the town. The local gossip only added fuel to the fire. She felt that the entire ordeal could be solved easily without her having to write something akin to *Unsolved Mysteries* - ban butter pecan cookies from the competition.

Seemed like a simple enough solution to her.

Shrugging her shoulders, January dropped the pen in her hand just as her mobile phone began singing in her purse. Blindly reaching into the sack, she griped the device and brought it to her ear. Only one person would call her while she was at work.

"Hi, Mom," January chirped, knowing that if she gave even the slightest hint of not being in the Christmas spirit, her mother would go to the ends of the Earth to change it.

She spent the next ten minutes piping into the conversation when it was expected. Listening to her mother explain how January's older sisters, April and June, had sent the cutest Christmas cards of their families and how she couldn't wait for Augustus to visit from his home in Montana, where he runs a ranch with his wife and their three kids.

Leave it to her mother to remind her that, as the youngest, she's the last one they get to see married off – it's her mother's Christmas wish. At least that's the guilt trip she threw January's way.

"Oh, and don't forget about decorating the family tree in two days when Augustus arrives."

Like she could ever forget.

"Yes, ma'am. I haven't forgotten in twenty-six years. Don't think I'll forget anytime soon."

"Don't you sass your mama, or I'll make your house look like the North Pole threw up there."

"I regret giving you a key now."

Chuckling, her mom added, "No, you don't, or you'd never have a stocked fridge."

"You're right," January lamented.

As the call began to dwindle, Samantha popped her head in to remind January about the interview that they had scheduled in thirty minutes.

"I have to go, Mom, but I'll see you on Thursday. I promise."

"I know, sweetheart. I'd love it if you had a special someone to bring with you. The more, the merrier."

The little dig at January's lack of love life stung. The last date she went on happened almost a year ago. It was slim pickings in Pineville. January supposed that she could try branching out to another town or attempting online dating, but neither seemed a great choice.

Ignoring her mother's jab, January ended the call after making another promise to be there Thursday.

Sliding her frame onto the cushioned chair behind her desk, January double-checked her family countdown on the calendar. Since she was little, her parents had created their own countdown to Christmas, including everything from a day to make cookies and gingerbread houses, to family night with a Christmas movie and going to the town Christmas parade.

She knew the schedule by heart – it never varied. You could always count on the list to remain the same.

A ping on her computer warned her of a calendar notification sent by Samantha. It was a preset alarm reminding her to pick out an ornament for her parents. It's the fourth one; she had been ignoring the previous alerts.

Of course, she had purposely ignored them, but as the days slipped away, she now had even less time to find the perfect gift for her parents. When January was five, she gave her parents a handmade ornament for Christmas, as did her siblings. Since then, she has given them one every year for their tree. It was an easy gift to find, and it definitely seemed to make her parents happy when they unboxed a piece of metal or glass covered in filigree.

A dark brown head of hair popped in from around the doorframe, reminding January that they needed to leave for the interview.

"I'll meet you out front in five. Oh, what is the name of that new shop in town with all of the Christmas things?" she questioned because she wouldn't have time to order the gift online, which was her usual MO.

"Nick's Knacks. We can stop by after the interview. It's not far from where we're meeting Ms. Davis and the volunteers for the Christmas Festival."

"Okay, great."

January thought about researching the shop online. It hadn't been in town but a few years, and if memory served her right, the older couple that ran the store retired here because of how much they loved the Christmas Festival. She had never stepped foot inside but knew that it carried a bit of everything.

Just as her hands hovered over the keyboard, she thought better of it. It seemed doubtful that a small shop like that would have an online catalog or store. She'd have to grin and bear it for a few minutes inside the shop until she found something her parents would love.

Four grueling hours later, January and Samantha walked away from their interview, sporting two completely different expressions. Samantha's face was lit up as bright as a star tree topper, whereas January's face looked as if she had eaten something sour with how tightly her lips were pinched together.

The festival committee had invited them to walk in the Christmas parade as elves around Santa's sleigh, a tremendous honor if Samantha's expression was anything to go by. Still, January would rather not be present at all.

"I can't believe we get to be in the parade!" Samantha joyfully exclaimed, her arms waving up and down as if she was about to take flight.

"Yeah." January's sarcastic tone earned her an eye-roll from her friend.

"You can at least pretend to be excited. No one will know it's you with the costume."

"And that should make me feel better?" January asked just as she stopped in front of a store with a wide window looking into a small Christmas village. "Is this the place?"

"Yep!" Samantha clapped her hands with a resounding cheer. "I can't believe you haven't been here before," she added as she held the door open for both women to enter.

"I do my shopping online and get it delivered in a day or two. Why do I need to go to a general store?"

January paused as she looked around the shop taking in the bags of mulch and gardening supplies lining the left wall and then housewares scattered along the right side of the building.

"What kind of place is this?" she mumbled to herself as she followed the brunette sprite toward the back of the shop. The leader bounced on her toes with each step that she took.

"This. ..this is heaven," Samantha explained with her arms open wide, showcasing the area.

January finally pulled her eyes away from the stacks of trinkets lining the end caps of the aisles and focused on the creation in front of her. Even though she hated Christmas, she couldn't deny the beauty of the wonderland fashioned at the back of the shop.

Fake snow fell from the ceiling, tumbling delicately onto the makeshift Santa's Workshop and the tree line of Firs and Pines. On the other side of the room, there were twenty or so decorated trees, each one covered in lights and themed ornaments. Each tree was given its own personality.

"Wow," the word dripped from her lips before she could catch them.

"Pretty impressive, huh?" a deep voice said from behind her, causing January to jump in surprise as she turned around.

What she found was no less impressive than the displays that had garnered her attention. A tall man with dark, almost black hair smiled warmly while balancing a large cardboard box in his well-muscled arms. Arms that stretched navy blue shirt sleeves to their limits.

With an apologetic smirk rising above his scruffy jaw, the mystery man murmured, "Sorry, I didn't mean to scare you." He adjusted the box in his grasp.

"It's okay. I'm usually not so easily distracted, especially not with Christmas displays."

He situated the box again and she asked if he needed any help, taking a step toward him.

"No, that's okay. Joey!" he shouted across the shop. It didn't take long for a thin teenager to step over to them. "Can you start unpacking these onto tree fourteen?"

"Sure."

"Thanks."

January watched as the teen quickly took the box from the mystery man's arms and carried it over to one of the decorated Christmas trees.

"Now," he stated, bringing her attention back to him. "Can I help you find anything?"

"You work here?"

January would never have imagined this rugged man with a hint of CEO running through his veins would be caught dead working at Nick's Knacks. He didn't have that down-home air about him. Instead, he reminded her of many of the men in high-profile positions that she has interviewed for the paper. The only local thing about this particular man was his pair of boots and worn-in denim jeans.

"For the time being."

Ah, so he is without a steady job, she thought to herself.

Or at least she thought she had said it to herself. His answering chuckle let her know otherwise.

"Actually, I'm a dentist by profession, but my grandparents run this place and asked for some help during the holidays."

With her spiked heel proverbially shoved into her mouth, January babbled, "Well, that's very. . ."

"Kind. Thoughtful. Considerate. Selfless. Any of those would fit nicely."

"Hmm. . ." she mumbled as she took a step toward the Christmas trees, leaving her friend to fend for herself in the Santa's Workshop.

January had hoped that she would be able to leave the conversation with some pride intact, but the stranger wasn't on board with that idea. He quickly followed in step behind her.

"You seem like someone that has come here with a purpose. Let me help, and I can get you out of the Christmas section before you break out in hives."

She tried to ignore him, but as she glanced down at her hands, she noticed that they were turning red and splotchy. The rest of her exposed skin most likely looked the same. January took a mental note to research being allergic to Christmas when she arrived home.

Quietly, she said, "An ornament," as she continued to take in each of the trees. There were classically decorated designs, beach-themed, some in a specific color, others using natural décor. Each was beautiful in its own way – as much as it killed her to admit.

She could feel the man's stare on her profile as he studied her. Admitting that he wasn't going to leave anytime soon, January wove an invisible white flag in surrender and turned slightly toward him.

"I get my parents an ornament for Christmas every year, and I forgot."

"What style do they have?"

She blinked at him as if he had just asked her to solve world hunger.

"Um. . .Christmassy? I don't know, I just find something shiny, and that's that."

The man chuckled at her response, which caused her already pink skin to flush in embarrassment.

"Let's stick with something classic then."

He gestured toward a tree in the far back corner that could have been a dead ringer for her parent's tree. She followed him toward the lush Fraser draped in red ribbon and white pearl garland.

January narrowed her eyes as she scanned each and every ornament, taking the time to walk around the tree twice until the perfect one came into her sight.

It was a delicate gold star inset with smaller stars. Nothing too fancy, but it would be a nice addition to their tree.

January opened her mouth without thinking and asked, "What about this one?"

January's mind was focused on finding the gift for her parents. She hadn't realized how close the man had been standing next to her. But with his new proximity, the smell of his cologne wafted beneath her nose. The sandalwood scent mixed with the fragrant smell of the tree left January in a haze until his arm brushed against hers as he pulled the ornament free from the branch.

"This is a beautiful piece. Good choice."

She was afraid she was mistaken, but their closeness also seemed to have affected him. His voice was deeper than before, grainier. In the stores back corner, it was almost as if they were in their own little world.

January looked up at him as he hung the star from his fingertips. "Thanks," she whispered, licking her lips out of habit. His eyes darkened as they followed the path of her tongue.

"There you are!" a perky voice shouted from around the tree, startling both January and the man, almost causing him to drop the gift.

"January, did you find anything?" she asked and then turned her gaze to the stranger, her eyes widening as she took him in. "You sure did," Samantha voiced without thinking.

Trying to diffuse the situation, January said, "Samantha, this is. . ." until she realized that she didn't know his name. Luckily, he chirped in and extended his hand. "Deckard."

"He was helping me find an ornament. He is the owner's grandson," she finished explaining.

Her friend's face fell slightly but then immediately reverted back to instant happiness as she took in the star ornament still dangling from Deckard's fingers.

"Come on," he suggested as he led them toward the registers. "I'll ring you out. Now, I can have this engraved with something special for you if you'd like. I can have it delivered tomorrow."

January paused for a moment before deciding it would be a nice touch. "Sure, just something generic is fine. Merry Christmas or Happy Holidays will work."

He rang up the gift and the additional charge for the engraving, and then the two women watched as Deckard tore off a green piece of paper and started making notations on the page.

"Okay, all I need now is a name and address for delivery," he asked expectantly.

"January Douglas at 5 Belle Street, Pineville, Ohio."

"Great. And now that I know your name and address, January, can I take you out for dinner tomorrow?"

She stared at him stupidly, wondering why this man would want to take out a Christmas grump like her.

"No, I have a boyfriend," she said, hoping to knock the cocky man off his pedestal. But instead of looking put off, he appeared more determined; the gleam in his eyes glared brighter as he met her steely gaze.

"No, she doesn't," Samantha chimed in, and January began to consider sending her friend's present back to the online store it came from.

Rolling her eyes, January adds, "I'm not interested."

"Yes, you are. Every woman within a ten-mile radius would be interested." but, of course, her best friend wouldn't let her off the hook that easily.

"Stop talking, Samantha," January chastised.

Deckard's hand covered his mouth to keep the chuckles from escaping. Turning her gaze back to the man, January added, "Sorry, I'm just busy the next couple of days."

"Well, if you change your mind, you know where to find me. I'm sure we'll run into each other during the festivities."

"Ugh, don't remind me," she loudly bemused as she turned herself and Samantha toward the door.

Calling out to her once more, Deckard said, "I'm hoping to see you soon, January Douglas."

With her hand pressed against the glass of the ajar door, January peered over her shoulder and did something completely unexpected.

She returned his smile.

RENEE HARLESS

Chapter Two

"I really need to learn to switch the station before I go to bed," she mumbled with her face pressed into the mattress as her pillow did little to suffocate the racket blaring from her alarm clock. Her morning was starting the same as it had the day before. Finally, she reached over and smacked the snooze button, ending the musical torture.

Just as she settled back into her pillow, the doorbell rang, and a guttural moan escaped from deep within her chest. January rolled out from under the covers and began shuffling at the pace of a sloth away from the bed still calling her name. The front door seemed farther away than she remembered.

The delivery driver usually didn't drop off at her house until the afternoon, but she supposed that he needed to start delivering earlier with the holiday season.

Without a single thought paid to her appearance as she passed the hall mirror, January ignored the way her bare legs were left exposed from beneath the oversized T-shirt that barely skimmed the underside of her butt. She didn't even care that her hair hung in a lopsided ponytail at the top of her head or that there were black smudges under her eyes from the makeup that never seemed to wash off completely.

Nope, she just didn't care since the only visitor she expected was the seventy-year-old delivery driver that had been with his partner longer than she had been alive. He wasn't going to ogle her. Plus, he had definitely seen her worse off. Like the time she had woken in a vomit-induced hangover after drinking herself silly the night before. Which was justifiable considering she had learned that her previous boyfriend was engaged three weeks after their breakup.

Her eyes remained closed as she twisted the knob to her front door, the cold metal against her palm doing little to wake January from her sleep-deprived mind.

"You're here early today, Chuck," January moaned as she opened the door wide and greeted the deliveryman.

"Not a morning person?"

Her eyes flew open in a flash at the sound of the voice on the other side of her porch. That sleep-deprived mind started flickering with memories of her attire, or lack thereof. January attempted to step back behind the door to cover her exposed legs, but her brain was still filled with haze. She ended up stumbling around her own feet until she tripped and landed on her backside, giving the attractive man from yesterday a spectacular view of her navy blue panties.

"You're a funny little thing, aren't you?" he joked as he tucked the small box under one of his arms and extended the other to help her off the floor. Not wanting to embarrass herself further, January accepted his help, but as her palm settled against his, she couldn't ignore the spark of awareness that zinged through her body at his touch. She wondered if he felt the same flicker of electricity, but January was too timid to ask. But when their eyes met, his darkened gaze gave her the answer.

"Um. . .yeah. . .mornings and I don't really get along. No matter how many hours of sleep I get, it always feels like zero. I even had a sleep study done and. . .I'm babbling." She tended to prattle on endlessly when she was nervous, which wasn't something that happened often, but with Deckard standing this close to her in her home and very little separating them, her mouth went off with a mind of its own.

Nervously she reached up to tighten the ponytail drooping on the side of her head but knocked her elbow into Deckard's chin instead.

"Oh gosh, I'm so sorry," she apologized as she tried to grasp his chin between her two palms. Not wanting additional injuries, Deckard clasped her wrists in one of his large hands.

"It's okay. I came by to bring your ornament. If I shipped it, the package wasn't going to arrive until Monday. This seemed like the easiest solution at the time. Though I wasn't prepared for bodily injury."

"You should always expect the unexpected with me." A stiff wind kicked up outside, hurling chilled air into her house. Shivers shot down January's limbs. "Um. . .do you want a cup of coffee or tea?"

Deckard let go of her wrists and stuffed his hands into his front pockets as he scanned her face, searching for something that left January's skin heated even with the cold air swirling around them.

"Yeah," he said, shocking her back into the moment. "That would be great, thanks."

She reached around him to shut the door, ignoring how her body was only a few inches away from his at the moment, and then gestured for him to follow her toward the kitchen. With an extra sway in her step, knowing that he was looking at her backside, she stepped down the hallway at a leisurely pace.

"Is this your family?" he asked.

Apparently, he wasn't looking at her bottom, after all, she thought.

"Yeah, that was from Christmas two years ago." Her parents had bought them all matching sweaters, even for the babies, and hired a photographer to snap a few hundred photos. She looked at the image over Deckard's shoulder, trying to see it from his perspective. Everyone looked perfect, happy, and excited - except her. She looked. . .

"You look miserable."

Yes, that was exactly right. She looked miserable because she was.

"I hate Christmas."

That had him spinning on his feet to look at her in astonishment.

"What? No one hates Christmas."

"I do," she told him as she turned away and walked back to the kitchen, hoping that the handsome but inquisitive man would follow. She grabbed two plain mugs from the cabinet and poured the coffee from the carafe.

"Cream or sugar?" she asked with her back turned to him as the sound of one of her barstools screeched along the hardwood floor. She scooped unhealthy mounds of sugar into her coffee, and after grabbing the creamer from her fridge within arm's reach, she poured a decent amount into her cup. She liked her coffee sweet and light.

"Black is fine," he replied.

January brought the other mug of coffee to her center island and handed it over to Deckard, but he wasn't going to let her free so easily.

"Tell me why you hate Christmas," he demanded, relenting his hold of her fingers on the mug handle.

"Don't you need to work?"

"I have time."

Under her breath, January murmured, "Of course you do." She didn't like to talk about why she hated Christmas. It was her burden and hers alone. And to most it would seem silly, but to her, it had been a problem that followed her around from day one, and she couldn't shake it.

"Would you believe me if I said it was because Christmas doesn't know how to stay in its own holiday realm? Like, why can't Christmas stay after Thanksgiving? I saw decorations before Halloween had even happened. I mean, what is that about?"

"While I don't disagree with you, I'm not sure that's why you hate Christmas."

For some reason, she wanted to tell him. She wanted to tell this gorgeous stranger that helped her find a last-minute gift for her parents and had done nothing but irritate her with his Christmas cheer. He did something to her that made her want to spill all of her secrets, the ones she kept buried deep inside, particularly the ones that January hadn't even shared with her best friend, Samantha.

"I can see you are thinking really hard over there," Deckard pointed out as he took a hearty sip of his coffee. "If you don't want to tell me now, maybe you can tell me over dinner tonight?"

"You're relentless, aren't you?"

Shrugging his broad shoulders beneath an olive-colored Henley, January failed to keep from rolling her eyes as he said, "I usually get what I want."

"And you want me?" she asked, not waiting to hear his answer as she dumped her drink into the sink and set the mug down. Boyfriends were bad news for January. She couldn't give them the attention they wanted, and most wanted it more than even she did. And with her distaste for the holidays, they usually found an excuse to stop coming around. So she stopped trying to date. There was no point. No one could love a Christmas grump. That's what her last boyfriend had said.

Just thinking about how he had dumped her the day after Thanksgiving and quickly found himself engaged just before Christmas irritated her more than Deckard being in her kitchen asking ridiculous questions. Anger began to roll off of January in waves.

"You really want to know why I hate Christmas?" At his silence, she continued as she stepped around to the other side of the island, putting space between them. "No one knows my birthday is December 24."

His eyes widened in shock at her confession, and she bit back a smug smile at Deckard's reaction.

Stuttering, he began to ask, "But your name is. . ."

"Yep." Completely irritated that she confessed something so personal, January turned her back on Deckard and moved toward her bedroom until her kitchen and Deckard were out of sight. "You can see yourself out," she shouted just before she slammed her bedroom door shut behind her.

It took January a full hour to calm down, dawdling like a toddler as she stood under the warm spray of the shower. She tried her damnedest to stop thinking about the man sitting in her kitchen, the complete stranger she had just blurted one of her darkest secrets to.

And it wasn't that the secret was all that deep and sinister, but nonetheless, it was a secret that she kept buried deep inside. It affected her life daily, not just hating Christmas but falsifying so much of herself to blend in with her family.

Finally, her skin turned into something resembling a wrinkled raisin and January forced herself to step free from the shower. She paused and took a deep breath, waiting to hear if any noise was coming from the kitchen. She couldn't hear much of anything, even with the exhaust fan turned off.

Slowly, January peered her head out around the bathroom door leading into her bedroom and found the room clear. She shuffled her towel-clad body over to her dresser. It took only a short time for her to tug on a pair of dark denim jeans and a loose cowl-neck sweater in a shade of bright red. Regardless of her feelings about Christmas, red was always one of her favorite colors, and as the sweater settled against her neck and shoulders, she couldn't help but bring the material up to her face and cuddle the soft cashmere.

She spent a few more minutes zipping her brown boots up her calves and swiping the wand of mascara across her lashes. Then she knew she had to face the music.

January quietly stepped out of her bedroom and down the hall into the kitchen. Knowing she had zero reasons to feel the pang in her chest as she took in the clean mugs resting on a drying rack beside the empty seat or the package Deckard had brought with him placed in the center of her kitchen island, her breath escaped her lungs anyway. He had done what she had asked – he left.

With a few minutes to spare before January needed to head toward the office, she took the small box off the counter and swiped her finger under the delicate gold sticker holding the top in place.

The soft white tissue paper protecting the ornament easily moved aside as she dipped her hand inside to retrieve the gift. Locating the string first, January unhurriedly tugged it out of the box, revealing the golden star in all its glory. The light coming from the kitchen window reflected off the corners of the metal while spun from her finger.

As it made its way in a full circle, January noticed the engraving on the backside of the ornament. It was a beautiful quote about a star of wonder that January remembered from one of the many Christmas carols her mother loved to sing.

"He had to pick a perfect quote, didn't he?" she asked herself aloud.

With a final glimpse at the delicate ornament, January pulled the tissue paper to the side, tenderly placing the ornament back in the packaging. But as she looked inside the small green box, a piece of glass caught January's eye, and she set the star on her kitchen counter.

"What the. . .?" January questioned as she gingerly lifted the weightless glass from the box.

She felt her mouth drop as she stared at the fragile ornament in her hand—a snowflake. January was so afraid that a beautiful, flawless glass snowflake would crumble in her grasp that her hand shook in fear.

Something began to tickle the back of her hand and she almost dropped the ornament until she realized that a small note was dangling from the ribbon tied through a hole at the top of the snowflake.

Make a wish

Say it twice

Close your eyes

And say goodnight.

When you wake

You will see

Just place this snowflake

On your tree.

January reread the note three times and still had no idea what it meant or why it was with her package, but she knew that it didn't belong to her.

"Deckard," she moaned just as her phone in the bedroom began to ring.

"Shit."

Doing her best to place the snowflake back in the box gently, she waited for it to settle before running toward the sound.

Tripping over her own feet in her rush to grab the phone before the call ended, January had to catch her breath before she could respond to the call.

"Hey," January said as she pressed the button on her phone to answer.

"Ms. Douglas, did you forget about the meeting this morning?" her boss, Mr. Roberts, asked with his signature tick sounding in his voice.

"No, sir." She had most definitely forgotten, but with Deckard making an unscheduled appearance this morning, her schedule was completely thrown out of sorts. "I'm on my way now. I'll be there before it begins." January ended the call before her boss could get in another word. Probably not the best decision, but it was too late to backtrack.

Grabbing the ornament box along with her purse and jacket, January shuffled out her door and drove toward Nick's Knacks, determined to return the snowflake back to Deckard and demand an explanation. But as traffic grew heavy on her way, she resigned herself to waiting until after her workday to track him down and give him a piece of her mind.

"He's on a tirade today," Samantha whispered as they both hurried into the conference room at the last minute. "And he wants to know where you are with the festival piece."

"Great," January groaned. Her day was quickly going downhill as fast as a snowball on a mountaintop.

After the four-hour meeting listening to her boss drone on about the upcoming articles and then another hour listening to him discuss the cruise he and his third wife were leaving for the next day, she was finally free. Or so she thought. As she ducked into her office to avoid the Secret Santa sign-up going around, she found a small gift sitting on her desk.

She knew what it was without even having to slip the lid of the box open. Her mother had a particular way of wrapping gift boxes. The top and bottom were always done separately, never together, then tied with a ribbon around the corners to hold it together.

It was another Christmas sweater. The tradition that hadn't waned in twenty-five years.

January knew she should call her mother to thank her for the gift and that she was sorry to miss her, but just as she sat at her desk, the phone rang.

"Hello, January Douglas speaking."

The rest of her afternoon went that way. Interviewees called to add some more information to their story, or members of the festival committee finally returned her messages. It was such a chaotic afternoon that she didn't have the opportunity to slip out for lunch. Instead, Samantha dropped off a sandwich, even going so far as to unwrap it for her.

When the clock at the bottom of her computer screen changed to 5:30 p.m., January slouched back into her chair with a heavy sigh. The day had been lost in a sea of phone calls and office visits. She barely had time to catch her breath, let alone make a run downtown to confront Deckard about the extra ornament.

"I'm heading out. Do you want to grab some dinner?" Samantha asked, even though January knew that Samantha had plans with her boyfriend.

"Thanks for the offer, but I actually need to run over to Nick's Knacks."

Samantha's face lit up and January knew what her friend was thinking.

"No, not to see Deckard. Well, I mean, I am going to see him, but it's because there was something wrong with the package he dropped off this morning."

"He was at your house this morning? He personally delivered the ornament?" she squeaked, sounding like a mouse being chased by a cat, but instead of fear, it was elation.

"Yes, but he was just being nice."

"Maybe you two can go out on that date he asked for yesterday." She smirked at her statement. A devilish grin spread across her lips.

"I don't want to go on a date with Deckard," January lied, even though she knew Samantha would be able to detect it. Whenever January wasn't telling the truth, she made non-blinking eye contact. She was the opposite of other people that diverted their attention away during a lie. January always looked someone dead in the eye. The no blinking tended to scare some people. It was her tell, and she knew it. So did Samantha.

And January had definitely fibbed because she couldn't deny that she was attracted to Deckard. He was the epitome of tall, dark, and handsome, with pale blue eyes that reminded her of the sky right after a snowfall. He made her heart and stomach flutter, which both elated and terrified her.

January bemused to herself, those darn butterflies had no business taking up residence.

What she wanted was to feel Deckard's strong arms wrapped around her and feel his smooth skin resting against hers. Feel the press of his full lips as they melded with hers in a heated kiss.

January could feel her cheeks flush at her inner thoughts, hoping that Samantha had missed it.

"I'm just going to ask him a question, leave, and heat up something in the microwave at home. Tomorrow, I need to pull out my box of ornaments from the attic for the tree decorating at my parent's house."

"Fine. I'll let it go this time. But I think you should give Deckard a shot. Think of how cute your babies would be?"

"Wow, you're definitely getting ahead of yourself. Plus, he's here to help his grandparents during the holidays. He's not staying in Pineville."

"But he could if someone that was kind and beautiful asked him to stay."

Chuckling to herself, January added, "Good luck finding her. I'll be leaving right behind you."

Samantha shook her long brown locks as she left the office and January did her best to tidy up her desk before heading out, but her mind was focused on the images of her and Deckard lying naked in her bed. It was just her imagination, but it was one heck of a fantasy.

~

The chime of a bell sounded as January stepped over the threshold of Nick's Knacks. The teenager from the other day stood behind the register ringing up a customer as January slipped toward the back of the store in search of Deckard.

She thought it would take a while to locate him, especially if he was in the back doing inventory or stocking up. But she should have known that he would be easy to spot. Deckard was standing next to Santa'smailbox handing out candy canes to the little boys and girls as they placed their letters in the red metal box.

January thought better of interrupting him, but as she took a few steps backward to obscure herself from his sight, she ran into the end cap of one of the aisles knocking down a display of snow scrapers.

She knew better than to look up at him as she tried to shove the scrapers back to their original placements, but for everyone she could get to stand up, another fell.

"Here, let me," his deep voice washed over her and January's breath caught in her throat.

"Thanks," she wheezed.

She watched as Deckard flawlessly stacked the scrapers back onto the end cap – not a single one tilted or appeared to fall. Even the pieces of plastic obeyed his command.

When every piece was aligned perfectly, they stood up in unison, and January was fascinated to see Deckard's eyes stray downward as if he was reserved. "I won't lie. I'm kind of surprised to see you right now."

Darn, I should apologize for this morning, January contemplated.

"I. . .uh. . .can be a bit moody in the morning."
There, that is sort of an apology.

As his eyes trailed up her body, they paused at the green box under her arm. In alarm, his gaze bolted up to hers. "Did you not like what I had engraved?"

"No!" she rushed. "I mean, yes. It was beautiful and perfect." January felt a sense of pride at being able to assure him that he had chosen well, and as his stiff body relaxed at her compliment, she felt her own body react. Except hers wanted to rip off the brown sweater and jeans the man was wearing.

"Then what brings you by?"

"I wanted to return the extra ornament you snuck inside."

"January, I don't know what you're talking about. What extra ornament?"

"The snowflake. I mean, it's lovely, but I can't accept it, Deckard."

His strong hand reached out, grasping her elbow and used his hold to steer her away from the children crowded around them. He was guiding her to the back corner of the tree display where they had met yesterday.

"I can assure you that I did not place a snowflake ornament in the package. And I'm the one that did the engraving, so no one else has touched that box."

"You did the engraving? Wow."

"Yes, with the help of a laser engraver. Now, focus. Can I see the ornament?"

Nodding her head, January opened the box and wrapped her fingers around the fragile piece. Slowly she brought it out of the box and let it rest on the palm of her hand.

"Wow," Deckard replied in amazement as he took in the glass ornament and his large fingers, reaching out to take it from her. January worried that he would break the delicate piece, but she should have realized that he would handle it with the utmost care. "This is magnificent. The glass is hollow on the inside, which keeps it so light. Someone spent a lot of time shaping this. You can see here by the wisps along the edges that it was hand blown. But the glass itself is flawless." She was in awe of him as he spoke of the snowflake as if it were a long-lost treasure. January couldn't tear her eyes away from him as he spoke.

His gaze traveled away from the snowflake and rested on her as he asked, "Where did you find this?"

"I didn't," she huffed. "That's why I'm here. It was in the box with the star."

"That can't be. It just can't. I packaged the entire thing myself. And believe me when I say, this piece was not in there."

"I don't understand," January whispered in complete shock.

Deckard turned his head to glance around at the trees on display, the snowflake still held within his grasp. She could see that he was looking to see if the ornament happened to fit alongside any of the other decorations, but they could both tell that it didn't belong on any of the trees. It was a piece of art that someone wouldn't find precariously placed on a branch. It would need a place of purpose. And that place wasn't in a general store.

"I guess I'll just take it home and put it on my tree."

"You could do that."

She could feel his eyes boring into her as she lightly took the snowflake from him and dropped it in the box, trying her damndest to ignore the sizzle from touching his skin.

"So, now that you know I didn't slip something so erroneously into your package, I suppose you will let me escort you to dinner tonight?"

"No way," she protested.

"Look, I don't want to pressure you or anything. But it's a free meal and I'm told I'm fairly good company."

"And how many women would say that?"

"My grandma? If you asked my ex-girlfriends, they would probably say differently."

January tried to hide her smirk. He was handsome, and she knew she felt an unnerving spark of attraction when he was close.

"Well. . . I suppose. . ."

"And you can tell me more about why you hate Christmas?" he probed.

"Fine. I guess I do owe it to you."

January felt her body recoil as Deckard softly pressed his hand at the small of her back to guide her from the store. It wasn't that she didn't want to feel Deckard's touch, but anyone's touch felt unfamiliar to her.

She could tell that Deckard felt her body flinch, and she murmured an apology, but January knew that her reaction only caused more questions.

He grabbed a dark gray wool coat on their way out the door and wrapped his large frame in its warmth as they stepped over the threshold. She thought better than to let him know that she had missed his touch already, but she didn't have to wait long before he seemed to miss touching her as well.

Deckard slid his hand down her arm to capture her free hand in his. Had anyone ever taken the chance to merely hold her hand, share a quiet strength with her? For some reason, January couldn't shake the feeling that if she needed someone, Deckard would be there.

"So, where are you taking me?" January inquired just as her stomach grumbled in response. Luckily, there were too many people milling about on the sidewalks for Deckard to hear.

"My grandmother mentioned a new sushi place a few blocks over. Is that okay?"

She was surprised he asked. Most men didn't care about her opinion on where to eat. She was more or less just a trophy on their arm – a pretty thing for them to look at.

"Sushi sounds great, actually. I don't go out to eat very often unless it's somewhere with Samantha, and she's not a very adventurous eater."

"Really? You seem like a worldly woman," Deckard pointed out as they waited at a crosswalk for the light to change.

"I wish. I get pretty homesick when I go away to follow a lead on a story. I work for the newspaper, by the way."

"I see. So leaving Pineville for, say, a boyfriend isn't something you'd be interested in?"

She looked up at Deckard after his assessment. His face didn't show any emotion except maybe a hint of curiosity.

"Um. . .I don't know. I've never given much thought to it, and I'd like to say that I'd follow my heart wherever it may take me. But honestly, you're probably right."

He squeezed her hand gently as they crossed the street toward the next block.

"Good to know," he said, then winked at her. Freaking winked with that same knowing smirk he had given her this morning. It had the same effect on her as watching a sexy man wear gray sweatpants. January wanted to see Deckard in a pair of gray sweatpants with nothing else on underneath. She was confident that he had that deep V-cut on his hips that guided onlookers to the best part of his maleness.

January's cheeks heated at her dirty thoughts of the man walking beside her just as snow flurries began to fall around them lightly.

"Tell me about where you're from," January prompted, trying to distract herself from her heated thoughts.

Deckard told her that he grew up in Atlanta, Georgia and that he had always wished to grow up in a small town like Pineville. When his grandparents moved up this way a few years back, he had been the first one to hop on a plane to visit them. He had fallen in love with the town at first glance.

His dental practice operated as a partnership, which he explained meant that he could always leave to open his own practice if he wanted. Deckard told her that was what he had been saving toward, but as he crept toward the age of thirty his mother had been on him to settle down.

"She would like you."

Curious, January asked, "Why do you say that?"

"Because you don't seem to be the kind of person to take shit from anyone. And from what I can tell, and what my grandparents have said, you're honest and caring. And quite beautiful." She blushed again, this time at his words and not at her internal musings. She didn't know what to say. Compliments always made her feel uncomfortable. Even when she won prom queen her senior year of high school, she barely looked up at the crowd when she crossed the stage to get her crown. "Hey, we're here."

"Thank goodness. I'm starving."

Together Deckard and January shared a platter of sushi and enjoyed a Japanese beer as they shared little anecdotes of their time as children. January felt that she shared more of herself than Deckard had. But it wasn't that Deckard was holding anything back. January could tell, based on her instincts, he just didn't have any thrilling stories as an only child. She had three other siblings, and as the youngest by almost ten years, she had numerous stories where hilarity ensued. He was an expressive listener, and she liked that about him. She also enjoyed watching his face morph with each story she divulged.

The sun had set a couple of hours ago and the snow had fallen steadily while they ate. As the server took away their plates, Deckard and January both glanced out the window and watched as the streets lit up with Christmas lights and decorations. Deckard's face morphed into utter happiness. His smile widened and his eyes began to sparkle. January witnessed it all in his reflection in the glass pane. Then she took in her own expression, her downturned lips with a slight snarl and her narrowed eyes. She was the complete opposite of Deckard. January silently wished that she could understand how Christmas could bring people so much joy and happiness – she had hated the holiday for so long that it seemed impossible to change.

"Hey," Deckard called out as he reached his hand across the table to grasp hers. "Want to talk some more about the bomb you dropped this morning?"

"Do I have to? It's not really something that I share with anyone."

"You never have to do anything you don't want to do, January, and I'd never force you to. But I like you and I'd like to know everything."

She liked him too. . .a lot, she just realized.

Taking a deep breath, January slipped her hand free from Deckard's, needing the space to garner some strength and ready herself for the ridicule she knew would come. Her reasons for hating Christmas were childish – she knew that, but she couldn't help it either.

Licking her lips, she thought she heard Deckard unsuccessfully biting back a groan as her tongue peaked out. It gave her only the slightest hint of satisfaction.

"Well, as I told you first, I hate that Christmas invades my favorite holidays. Holidays that specifically involve food and dressing up. I also hate that my favorite music stations start playing Christmas music incessantly the minute Thanksgiving is over – sometimes even sooner. And yes, I know that I could find a new station or listen online, but that's not the point. I shouldn't have to." Deckard smartly remained silent as January continued her rant. She was on a roll now and didn't want any interruptions. "And the forced cheer. Ugh. I am automatically typecast as a grump or Scrooge if I'm not filled with Christmas cheer twenty-four-seven. I am called a bitch if I decline holiday parties because I'm not festive.

"And with my family, the Christmas cheer has to be turned on at all times, and to be honest, it's exhausting."

"I'm sorry, January. What about your birthday?"

"I'm getting there. I just need a minute."

In her mind, she's reliving her childhood - the teasing, name-calling, and lies. All of it was painful and made her chest ache. It took her closing her eyes and shutting herself away from the world that she found the courage to continue.

"I have three siblings with names matching their birth months. June, April, and Augustus. My brother was the youngest and my parents were done having kids until I surprised everyone when my brother was nine.

"My mother was elated, she always wanted a big family, and another child was a miracle in her eyes. My due date was for January thirteenth and my parents were tickled to be able to name me January. They had everything monogrammed and had started referring to me by my name from the day they learned my gender. To them, it was a sign.

"But there were complications and I was born three weeks early – on Christmas Eve. My mother almost died giving birth to me and I would have ruined my entire family's Christmas. My brother and sisters had to spend Christmas night at the hospital with my parents, all praying that my mom lived. Then when she pulled through, they realized that Santa had missed them. There was no Christmas that year.

"I know my parents don't blame me for it, but my siblings did for a long time, and I did too."

Chiming in, Deckard said, "January, none of that was your fault. You were an innocent baby. Sometimes bad things happen. And I'm sure it was simply an accident that your parents forgot to have gifts ready under the tree."

January was too deep into her self-loathing that she barely heard his consolation. She continued, "The teasing and name-calling started when I began kindergarten. I was excited that my birthday fell the day before Christmas, even though it was almost impossible to celebrate because Christmas overshadowed everything. But I was little and didn't understand. I always thought the hubbub was for me, you know?

"The kids would say that my parents were dumb and didn't know their months, or they would call me a mistake. And my parents tried their hardest to make sure that I had my own little celebration for my birthday, but classmates and family could never come because they were off on a break or doing their own Christmas festivities. When I turned seven, my parents stopped trying to throw parties because they could see how much it hurt me to have no one attend. It was hard.

"As I got a little older, I started to despise the holiday more and more."

"I'm sensing this isn't the end of the story," Deckard stated.

"Not even close," January snickered coldly. "My oldest sister is about fourteen years older than me. She and her boyfriend got engaged one summer and wanted a winter wedding – the weekend before Christmas that year, on winter solstice.

"My tenth birthday was coming up and all I wanted was a Barbie Dream House. I was a little too old to be playing with them, but I didn't really care what anyone thought of me at that point. I didn't have many friends.

"Anyway, I had been dropping hints like crazy all year that the house was what I wanted for my birthday. But my parents were so absorbed with the wedding and Christmas that they forgot."

"They didn't get you the Dream House?" Deckard asked.

"They didn't get me anything. My entire family forgot my birthday that year. So, I stopped celebrating. And when I went to college, I began telling everyone that my birthday was in January whenever someone asked."

"Damn," the man sitting across from her mumbled, dumbfounded.

"The thing is. . .I love winter. I think it's beautiful, especially here in Pineville. I love the snow and I love the quiet that comes with it." January said, grunting at her own assertion, "I bet you think I'm crazy."

Opening her eyes, she peered across the table at him and she was surprised at what she saw. Deckard didn't appear to pity her as she had imagined. No, he seemed angry. His jaw cracked as he ground his teeth against each other and his right eyebrow seemed to have acquired a twitch.

"Deckard, are you okay?" she asked as she reached for the same hand that had held hers earlier.

January was glad when he gripped her hand in return. She was afraid that voicing her feelings would have him running for the hills or trying to change her mind as others had done in the past. But Deckard's expression was far from one she had seen before. He appeared angry and January didn't understand why.

"I just. . . I get it and I wish that there was a way I could fix all of that for you. And most of all? I'm so damn angry at your family that I can barely remain sitting here and not storm off toward your parent's house and give them a piece of my mind."

"That's sweet of you, Deckard. But you don't need to fight my battles. I'm sure my family felt bad enough."

"Well, someone should."

She felt awkward having this man she barely knew feel as if he needed to justify her feelings, but at the same time, it felt good. Like, she wasn't alone anymore. And Deckard was definitely someone she wanted to have around more often, despite Samantha's ribbing.

"It's okay, Deckard."

"It's not," he proclaimed, then his face morphed back into the masculine softness it had been while they enjoyed dinner together. "I just want you to know that I understand no and I don't blame you for how you feel, but there are a lot of special things about Christmas. Like, being with family and those you love. Kissing under the mistletoe with someone special when no one is looking, watching kids tuck themselves into bed hours early as they wait for Santa's arrival, I could go on and on."

She wished that he would. January was hypnotized watching his lips move up and down as he spoke, and she craved to feel them brush against her bare skin.

Even though he tried to stifle back his frustration by overshadowing the bad with the good, January could see he was losing the battle.

"Are you ready to go?" she asked, trying to give him an out. "I probably ruined your night with my rant."

Deckard cocked his head as he listened to her speak. "I don't think you could ruin anything, January. Especially not with me."

"I wish that there was something I could do to change your mind," he said, slipping out of the booth and holding out his hand for hers. January willingly placed her hand back into his and she marveled at how right it felt. "Don't forget the box," he prompted as she almost left it sitting on the table.

"Thanks," she acknowledged, grabbing the package and tucking it under her arm once again, still wondering how and where the glass snowflake had come from.

Together they walked hand in hand back to the public parking lot where January had parked her car on her way to Nick's Knacks. There was a biting chill in the air, but it wasn't unbearable.

She offered to walk alone as they passed Deckard's family's shop, but he vehemently declined to allow her to walk alone. He explained that he wasn't only a gentleman but also wanted to spend a few minutes with her.

January knew at that moment that she would fall for Deckard, and it would be hard and fast – a complete whirlwind.

She wished she could press a pause button as her car came into view, but she knew their time was up.

"This is me," she said as she sidled up next to the car and placed her bag and the gift box on the roof. "Thank you for dinner. And sorry for the accusations earlier."

"Don't mention it. And I want to thank you for telling me everything." His free hand crept toward her face until the pads of his fingers brushed across her cheek. January expected his touch to be rough against the sensitive skin of her face, but she was surprised to be met with a tender softness. "Maybe you'll let me help you celebrate your actual birthday this year."

"It's Christmas Eve, I'm sure you'll be preparing for the big day."

"I'd rather be with you," Deckard whispered as his fingers slid back and forth delicately across her cheek. She could feel herself falling within the depths of Deckard's spell. What he possessed was potent and powerful, and January was hypnotized. "Can I take you out for dinner again before then?"

January wanted to say yes. She wanted to shout it from the rooftops, but then her parent's ridiculous Christmas schedule galloped through her mind leaving a trail of heavy footprints on her heart.

"I'm not going to be free for a while. My parents have this crazy schedule that starts tomorrow leading up to Christmas. My brother and sisters are all coming into town," she tried to explain, her words speeding up as she spoke. "Maybe we can do something after the holidays?"

The pit in her stomach intensified as she watched his face morph into dejection.

"I can't, January. I'm leaving on Christmas after breakfast with my grandparents. The shop is closed."

The feel of his touch on her cheek and neck ceased to exist. January could only feel the pinch of coldness as it swirled around them, nipping away at every ounce of happiness she had been feeling.

"I'm sorry," she whispered. "I could maybe –"
January was interrupted by Deckard as he pressed his lips against hers, silencing her words. The softness of his kiss had every thought escaping January's mind.

The parking lot drifted away, and all January could see was Deckard as he pulled back. His eyes were heavy with desire and fire swirled in his irises as he took in her swollen lips.

January couldn't hold herself back. Her heart was pounding in her chest as she reached for the lapels on Deckard's coat and tugged him closer, yearning to explore his mouth fully.

Deckard didn't fight her need for him. Instead, he reached down and lifted her up, pressing her back against the car door. She instinctively wrapped her legs around his waist, not giving a single care if anyone saw them. Their chemistry was so explosive January feared if anyone dared to come close to them at that moment, they would get burned.

She loved the way he tasted. A bit like the beer they had enjoyed during dinner and a trace of the after-dinner mints the server handed them after their meal. It was an odd combination but she liked it just the same – because it was Deckard's kiss that she couldn't get enough of.

"Tomorrow." *Kiss.* "Lunch." *Kiss.* "Noon." *Kiss.* "Pick me up."

"Where?" He trailed his kisses away from her lips down to her neck, sucking on the sensitive skin, causing her limbs to shiver.

"The Newspaper offices on Third Street."

"Okay," Deckard said as he pulled his mouth away from her neck and gazed adoringly at her. He brushed his lips against hers once more as if he couldn't restrain himself but pulled back before she could bring them back to the heated passion they had found themselves in moments ago.

The hold on his control began to waver as he growled, "I should let you go." January almost laughed as she felt his grip on her bottom tighten, but disappointment quickly blossomed when his fingers loosened and she slipped down his body until her feet landed on the ground.

January felt bereft as he took a step back, adding space between their two bodies. Embarrassment flushed her cheeks at how she pawed at him shamelessly. Control wasn't something that January ever lost. She always kept it in check. But she had tunnel vision. There was nothing else at that moment but her and Deckard. She wondered if that was how they would be if they were able to see where things may go, but he was leaving. Soon. As in nine days.

It was going to hurt. She knew that. Because even though Samantha teased her about being attracted to Deckard, once the feelings settled, they blossomed and bloomed at an alarming rate until they wove around each and every muscle and bone in her body.

Love was going to come swiftly if January didn't keep her emotions locked away.

And when Deckard placed his curved index finger under her chin to tilt her face toward his, January knew fighting their attraction was going to be a lost cause. In just two short days, she knew the inevitable would happen. Now she had to figure out a way to keep it from hurting too badly when he left.

Deckard sealed his lips over hers once more and wished her a good night as she slipped into her car. As she drove away, January peered into her rearview mirror and watched as he stood stoically in the spot she had just vacated, his hands tucked into his coat pockets and a smirk gracing his lips.

January didn't think that there was anything that could ruin her night. It was a perfect date that she had been so hesitant to go on after the last boyfriend debacle. Even though Deckard used a guilt trip to have her join him, she didn't fight that hard. Her attraction to him left her with tunnel vision.

Pulling up to her house, she was too lost in her memories of kissing Deckard that she missed the Christmas lights strung around the banister of her porch or the white light-up snowman in the yard. It wasn't until she stepped inside her house that reality struck.

Now, not only did she have a Christmas tree in her house, but she had a mantle covered in a Christmas village and garland. Stockings hung in front of her fireplace. More garland draped around her kitchen island, and the doors in her house were wrapped to look like presents.

It looked like someone had come into her house and created her worst nightmare.

Thoughts of Deckard quickly disappeared from her mind as anger grew in their wake. She ripped the wrapping paper off the doors first, balled it up, and threw the scraps in the trash. Next to go were the garland and bows in the kitchen. For every tied bow she had to unravel or taped garland she had to peel away from the granite, her temper rose until January swore she saw red.

She hated that her mother felt that she could force January to partake in anything Christmassy. It was bad enough that every night for the next nine days was going to be overrun with the dreaded holiday cheer that she hated. January wished she could back out of the traditional events; she had even tried before, but that secret yearning to make her parents happy was always present. And there was nothing she could do to tamper that feeling. Seeing them happy made her happy, always.

When January got to her fireplace, she couldn't bring herself to dismantle the Christmas village; it was her mother's old set, the one she used to admire as a little girl. She would spend hours watching the little magnetic figurines move along the streets or skate on the plastic ice.

The heaviness of the moment settled on January's shoulders and her anger began to dissipate.

"Damn," she murmured, walking over to the couch and settling on the cushions. Looking around her living room, January decided she could deal with how it looked until Christmas, and then she could take it all down the minute she woke.

From the corner of her eye, the green gift box caught her attention and she reached over to the coffee table to grab it.

Now she wished she hadn't left the star ornament on her kitchen counter, but it wasn't her fault that her mother ruined the surprise of the gift.

Opening the lid, January reached inside, lifted the snowflake from its confines, and read the inscription once again.

"Make a wish, huh?" she asked aloud.

"Well, I wish that there was no Christmas. I wish that Deckard wasn't leaving. I wish that we had a chance to see where things could go. I wish my mother would stop barging into my house when I'm not home," she said as if asking a genie to grant her three wishes.

January heard her phone chime in her bag and she blindly snatched it. A message flashed on the screen

Samantha: Meant to tell you that I signed us up for the secret Santa gift exchange.

Great, she thought as she tossed her phone back on the couch.

Remembering the snowflake still resting in her palm January stood from the couch and marched toward the small table beside the Christmas tree where she hid all the Christmas cards she had received. With a tug, the drawer opened and she placed the snowflake on top of the papers, then prepared to shut it. But then sadness pushed through her at the thought of hiding such a beautiful piece that someone painstakingly crafted. It didn't deserve to hide away in a drawer.

Slipping the ribbon between her fingers, January carried the piece to the Christmas tree and found a branch along the top that was still bare.

Quietly January whispered, "I wish there was no Christmas," and placed the ornament on the tree, rolling her eyes at the small piece of paper hanging on the ribbon as it caught her eye.

"My wishes never came true before and I seriously doubt they'll start now," she said skeptically to the empty room as if the snowflake would answer.

With a deep breath, January turned off the lights around her house, grabbed her phone, and got herself ready for bed.

As she stripped herself free of her clothes, she dove under the sheets, not even caring that she was only wearing a pair of panties.

Her phone pinged with another message.

Unknown: Hope you got home okay. This is Deckard, btw.

She immediately hit reply.

January: Came home to a nightmare. Will tell you at lunch. How did you get my number?

Deckard: Your friend came by the store and gave it to me.

January didn't know what to think. She was angry with Samantha for giving Deckard her number, but she supposed she should have given it to him herself. And if it wasn't for Samantha, January may not have realized that she really *did* want to date Deckard.

At her pause, another message came across.

Deckard: Don't be mad. She meant well.

January: I'm not. Just getting ready for bed. Tired from all the excitement tonight.

Deckard: I had a good time too. Get some rest. I'll see you tomorrow.

January: Goodnight.

Deckard: Sleep well.

As January closed her eyes, she knew that she would do as Deckard wished. Her mind was running playback of her night with him, and as she fell asleep, she had a smile grace her lips.

RENEE HARLESS

Chapter Three

January rolled over in bed and slapped at the alarm clock radio with a flailing arm, wishing that she had five more minutes to finish the dream between her and Deckard.

The music seemed louder this morning, and as she pried her eyes open to figure out the time, dawning fell on January. The radio wasn't playing a Christmas carol or commercial. No, it was blaring one of her favorite songs from the summer.

"Huh?" she wondered as she sat up in bed, grabbed the radio, changed the stations, and listened carefully as she flipped through.

"No," she gasped. Rushing out of bed, her feet tangled in the sheets, and she fell headfirst out of her bed, smashing her face against the hardwood floors. But she didn't feel the pain. She felt panic instead.

Running out of the bedroom clad in just her panties, January didn't even bother to check to see if her window coverings were closed. Her bare feet pounded down the hallway, and at the opening, she stared in shock at her living room. There wasn't a single remnant of Christmas in the space. Not a bow, not a light, not even a broken pine needle from the tree. The room was empty.

"Oh no," she gasped. "Oh no. Oh no. Oh no. What did I do?"

January felt faint. Her mind whirled and she stumbled over to the couch to sit, tucking her head between her legs as her mom used to show her. The walls continued to feel as if they were closing in and January struggled to catch her breath.

She couldn't believe that she made that stupid wish last night, and now she's deprived an entire world of a joyous time simply because she had been wronged as a child.

It can't be real, she thought. January was sure her parents were playing a prank on her. They knew how much she wanted nothing to do with the holiday.

Pushing away from the couch with new resolve, January sprinted back to her room, tugged on a sweatshirt, and slipped on her fur-lined boots. She was glad she always kept around an oversized sweatshirt as this one hung down to her knees.

With heavy steps, January left her bedroom and walked right out her front door. She almost slipped as she dashed down the stairs to her yard.

The snowman out front was gone, as was the string of lights. But January's stomach dropped as she took in her neighbor's houses. Her head turned to the left, then right, then left again – everything was bare.

No red and green. No lights. No giant inflatable lying dormant on the ground. It was all gone.

January's breath began to catch again in fear, but a voice sounding from the sidewalk had her spinning on her heels and almost falling on her butt in the cold snow.

"If this is how you greet everyone in the morning, I'm likely to get jealous."

"Deckard," she spoke softly. Tears pooled along her lower lids as the gravity of what had transpired began to settle. She needed someone and he was here at the perfect moment.

She scurried toward him and January threw her arms around his waist as she let her emotions get the better of her. January hadn't even noticed the two paper cups he held in his grasp as she fell into him.

"Oh my gosh, Deckard. It's all gone. Everything. And it's all my fault."

"What? Were you robbed, January?" Deckard asked, now on high alert as he looked around her yard.

Confused, she looked up at him and tilted her head with furrowed brows. "No. Christmas. It's all gone."

Deckard's shoulders sagged in relief that she hadn't been robbed. His arm loosely wrapped around January's shoulders as he tried to guide her back into the house, the coffee cups still in his hands.

"Let's get you inside, okay? You're going to catch a cold out here with no pants."

"Deckard, I'm serious." She tried to pull herself away from him, but he tightened his arms protectively.

"So am I, January. Your neighbors are starting to watch. Let me get you inside and we can talk, okay?"

January looked around and noticed that everyone had started filing out of their houses and were taking in her display. She knew she had been yelling frantically, but she was completely freaked out.

"And as much as I hate it, let's get some pants on you."

She let him guide her inside the house, setting their cups on the kitchen island as they passed. Deckard followed her into her bedroom and she watched him look around the gray and cream room as she tugged on a pair of boxer shorts.

"Am I supposed to feel better with you wearing another man's boxers?"

January wanted to laugh, but her mind was too preoccupied with wondering what was going on to care.

"Sorry, they're comfortable to sleep in. Can we figure out what the hell is going on before I have another panic attack, please?"

He nodded as he dutifully followed her from the bedroom into the living room, watching her pace back and forth along her rug.

She was murmuring to herself about the Christmas tree, the ornament, and how someone was playing a cruel joke on her.

"Want to explain to me what's going on before you wear a hole in your rug?" he suggested as he placed both of his hands on her shoulders. The touch was soft and placating, like he was trying to keep her from running away.

"I'm not crazy, Deckard."

"I know you're not, sweetheart. But you're freaking out right now and I want to understand why."

"It's gone. Christmas. I wished it away last night and it happened."

"Christmas?"

"Yes!" she shouted, trying to get him to understand.

"I don't know what Christmas is. Is it a pet, like a cat? Did it get loose?"

"No! Gah!" she cried out, commencing her pacing.

"Christmas is a holiday that happens on December twenty-fifth. It's a religious holiday and a commercial one. There are presents, and parades, and Santa, and I ruined it all!" January felt like she was growing more hysterical as every second lapsed, and Deckard stared at her in confusion.

"Okay, let's have a seat and you can tell me more about it. It sounds like the town's winter solstice festival in a few days."

He ushered her to the couch and she willingly sat with his help. January was afraid that she was losing her mind or had already lost it.

"Deckard," she asked, licking her now dry lips, "How did we meet?"

"You don't remember?"

"Obviously, I'm second-guessing everything," January snarled.

"Maybe you hit your head last night. You seemed fine after dinner."

Urgency pulsated in January's veins and she prompted Deckard again to answer how they met.

"Well, you came in the shop with your friend and were looking for a gift for your parents for the winter solstice celebration. You chose a beautiful gold star."

"Wow. Okay. So how we met is exactly the same, but the reasoning is different. Winter solstice is on December twenty-first, right?"

"Yes. And we went to dinner last night, and you unloaded on me your reasons for hating the winter solstice because it overshadowed your birthday on the twenty-fourth."

"Damn," January mumbled as she looked around her living room in despair. Everything was lining up the same, but she knew with complete certainty that it was all wrong.

"Do you think I'm crazy, Deckard?" she whispered as she looked over at him. Without pause, he replied, "Not at all. You seem really shaken up over this and I can see the honesty in your eyes. Tell me what happened."

January sighed in relief. He believed her, or at least wanted to believe her.

Taking a deep breath, she launched into the last two days, not leaving out a single detail. She told Deckard about the snowflake and how she had stupidly made a wish on it, and hung it on her Christmas tree that sat in the corner, then went to bed. His eyes widened with each sentence and she was almost afraid he was going to have her committed to an asylum at any moment.

"Wow, that's. . .uh. . .something."

"I'm not lying, Deckard. It happened, I swear to you. People have been celebrating Christmas for eons."

His touch instantly calmed her hysterics, placing his hand on top of hers. "Don't get worked up again. I believe you. Let me help you. Maybe we can figure out what is going on. You're a reporter, right? Do you think we can look through some old papers or something?"

"Oh my gosh, you're a genius!" she exclaimed, placing her hands on the sides of his face and pulling him close. She smacked a quick kiss on his lips before jumping up from the couch.

"I'm going to take a quick shower and then we can get to work," January shouted as she began to back away, but then turned to look over her shoulder at Deckard, who had started to slouch back against the couch. "Thank you, Deckard. For trusting me."

"January, I really like you. Even if we are only ever friends, I will always trust you."

Nodding her head, January made her way back to her bathroom, praying that she doesn't let either of them down. And she wasn't just thinking about Christmas.

At record speed, January finished her shower and dressed. By the time she stepped back out into the hallway, only ten minutes had elapsed. As her soft steps carried her into the living room, she found Deckard no longer on the couch but sitting on one of her barstools, sipping one of the cups he had brought. He was speaking on the phone, and January didn't want to interrupt or eavesdrop, but she couldn't help herself.

"No, Gram. I'm really worried. Something's happened and it's really affecting her. I'm going to spend the day helping her figure it out. I'll be back to work tomorrow, Gram, but maybe keep my evenings free. Yeah, I really like her. I love you too."

As he ended the call, January stepped into the kitchen and snatched the other cup Deckard had brought.

"So. . ."

"I knew you were there. I could smell your perfume."

Dang. So much for incognito.

"Where are we headed first?" he asked as he took a final sip from his cup and placed it in the trash can at the end of the island.

"The archives. They'll have everything I can search through."

"Sounds good. Let's go."

The wind swirled around them as they stepped outside, kicking up the ends of January's scarf, and tickling her nose. Deckard pressed his key fob, and January didn't want to argue about who would drive, so she wordlessly followed him toward his car.

They drove in silence and as they approached the newspaper's building. Grabbing her badge from her bag, January scanned it at the front desk, while taking note that the lobby wasn't covered head-to-toe in holiday decorations. Instead, stars dangled from the two-story ceiling in celebration of the solstice. Deckard followed her down the steps toward the basement where they kept the old published papers and January prayed that many of them had been scanned into the electronic database. If not, that made their task much more difficult.

There was a line of computers against the furthest wall and January headed in that direction first, Deckard trailing on her heels.

"Here, you run a search on the word Christmas," she typed on the screen in front of him, "and I'll search for some of the other lingoes regarding the holiday. We're bound to come up with something."

But two hours later, both of their searches came up short. The closest recognition January could find was regarding Saint Nicholas, who was a real person. There was no mention of the holiday, Santa, or even any of the other religious connotations regarding the Christmas celebration. It was as if the entire holiday had never existed.

Pushing away from the desk, January slumped in the office chair in defeat.

"I just don't understand. I didn't make it up, Deckard. It was a holiday that meant so much to so many people. It couldn't have disappeared."

Deckard looked at her with pity and she hated that feeling of questioning herself. She couldn't blame him. Even to January, her story was beginning to sound a bit far-fetched.

"Hey, we still have a list of sections that seem to ping a few articles that we can look at. We just need to search through the shelves," he pointed out.

"Yeah, okay."

Dust filled the room as they went through a few boxes of older papers, many dating back to when the town of Pineville came to be. There were mentions of a religious celebration on December 25, but nothing specifically related to Christmas.

Everything regarding town-wide festivals was centered around the winter solstice. She could see where the Christmas celebrations she had hated for so long had been changed into a different theme.

She frantically sifted through more and more boxes, not finding anything to ease her frustrations. January was close to tossing each and every paper into a pile in the corner in her haste to find an answer.

"Hey, hey. Calm down," Deckard consoled with a soft touch on her arm.

"Deckard, I. ..I just don't understand."

He pulled her away from the box of papers she had been sorting through and held her in his arms, trying to ease her disappointment by taking it into himself. He was prepared to be her anchor and she was willing to allow him to act like it.

Because though he wasn't saying it, she was afraid she had gone crazy.

"Come on, sweetheart. We've been here for three hours. Let's grab some lunch and maybe we can get some clarity."

"Maybe. . ." she began to say, doubt seeping into her skin, causing her to question herself.

"Don't, January. I believe you. If there was something special that we ae missing out on, I want to know all about it. Maybe it will help."

"Yeah," she murmured against his chest as he held her close. His hand rubbed up and down against her spine, leaving trails of heat across her back. January allowed his touch and smell to soothe her.

Together they walked away from her office toward the bakery across the street. The air smelled like snow and cookies and January closed her eyes to take a deep breath. Deckard was careful not to bring up any of the celebrations coming up in the town, but as they stepped inside the eatery, two of her co-workers approached and asked if she still planned on being in the solstice festival with Samantha.

January floundered; she couldn't be in a celebration that she knew nothing about. She vaguely remembered that Samantha had signed them up to be in the Christmas parade when she interviewed the group running the festival. This must be a different version. It seemed like she was living in an alternative universe.

Noticing the horror on her face, Deckard wrapped an arm across her shoulders and tugged her body against his. "Actually, January is going to have to decline the participation in the celebration. She'll be observing the solstice with my family this year."

The jaws on their faces collectively slackened, forming large gaping holes just below each of their noses.

"It's a new development," January chimed in, hoping that she didn't sound as freaked out as she felt with Deckard holding her so close.

Using the firm hand on her shoulders, Deckard steered them toward a table in the corner and kept her back facing the door. He offered to grab them both a sandwich from the counter and she nodded in thanks.

Delving her hands into her bag, the metal of a spiral spine bit at her palm and she gripped her notebook, pulling it out of its confines. The pages flipped through her fingers until she landed on the page of the religious celebrations that were still eminent during the season. She skimmed through the scribbles and then turned to a blank page just as Deckard sat back down with a tray of sandwiches and two cups of water.

"So, how do we celebrate Christmas?"

January paused while lifting the large club sandwich toward her mouth, a piece of turkey dangling from between her fingers.

"Well, Christmas began as a cultural and religious holiday, and I suppose that it was still celebrated in that aspect. But it picked up as a commercial holiday around the 1940's, or that's what many people claim. There was a movie called *Miracle on 34th Street* that many people say launched Christmas into a new stratosphere. Since then, it's only become more and more commercialized. Presents and their worth tend to overshadow everything people used to love about the holiday."

Deckard looked at her fondly, his kind eyes listening to her every word, but with a wrinkle knotted between his brows as if he was trying to figure her out.

"What?" she asked as she took a hearty bite of her sandwich, loving how the simple flavors burst in her mouth.

"I'm just trying to figure something out. You appear truly distraught over this holiday no longer in existence, but your lips curled in revulsion with every word you spoke.

"So, I'm trying to figure out what you actually miss about it. I remember you explaining why you dislike the solstice celebration, is it the same for Christmas?"

It hadn't occurred to January that her conversations up to this point would have remained the same, just with different reasoning.

"So, I told you everything? My birthday, the wedding, all of it?"

"Don't you remember?"

Slouching back in her chair January truly felt as if she was losing her mind. She wasn't sure which way was up, which way was down, or even what had happened before today.

"I think I do, but everything is such a jumble right now." Then the kiss from last night popped into her head and she remembered how it left her panting in the parking lot.

Leaning forward, January whispered, "We. . .um. . .did we kiss last night?" She hated to ask so bluntly, but it was such a perfect kiss that she felt as if she would die if he said no. Her palms began to sweat as she waited breathlessly for his response. January had some wild dreams in the past and she absolutely didn't want this one to be a dream.

At first, she thought he was going to play coy and not reply, but he answered with a nod before leaning forward in the booth. His elbows perched on the table and he drew one of his strong fingers across his bottom lip. January was mesmerized by the movement and couldn't pull her stare away, no matter how hard she fought against it.

She tried to look away and failed - until he started speaking, then she found herself falling further down the rabbit hole. "We did and it was the hottest kiss of my life. And I'd really like to do it again. Soon."

She sat there, slack-jawed. And January was almost positive her cheeks were the same color as the red tablecloth.

"Now, tell me why you miss Christmas. Not what everyone else is missing out on. But what *you* miss. Was there anything you liked at all?"

The question left her speechless. Reasons for liking the holiday left her memories many years ago, but she realized something as she sat and pecked away at her sandwich. January recognized that while she hated how much Christmas had overshadowed so many special times in her life, it brought happiness to so many others, especially her parents. They loved the holiday and all the hubbub associated with it. But most of all, they loved being with family.

January's mother had her Christmas traditions that, to January, forced her to participate in things she had no desire to do, but she did it because she knew that it made her mom happy. And if her mom was happy, her dad was happy.

Pushing the empty plate to the edge of the table, she grabbed her pen and started scribbling in her notebook.

"So, every year since I can remember, my mom did her own personal countdown. It wasn't something like marking days off a calendar. We did something special on certain days leading up to Christmas Day."

"Okay. What kind of things? Maybe they do something similar to the Pineville Winter Solstice Celebration."

Continuing to write out the countdown she remembered for this year, January didn't look up from her paper as she mumbled, "Maybe."

Finally, she stopped writing and gazed down at the paper before her. Images of the previous year's events flashed in her mind.

"Want to share what you wrote down?" Deckard asked. Her head jerked upward at his question and she had to shake her head to free it of her memories.

"Yes, sorry." She handed over the notebook to Deckard's waiting hand and he started scanning it over, his eyes moving with each word on the page

"So, this is ten days out?" At her nod, he continued, "Day one: decorate Christmas tree?"

"Yes, so we would go find the perfect pine tree and decorate it with beautiful glass ornaments, lights, garland, and tinsel that have been passed down in my family for years. There used to be a tree lot here in town, but I'm guessing that isn't the case anymore. Your grandparent's store had a beautiful Christmas display with differently decorated trees.

"Every year, I brought an ornament to place on my parent's tree. It was really special. It was something we did as a family. Most of my siblings forgot through the years, but I remembered every year. My mom always had what we called her pretty tree. It looked like something out of a magazine. She loved Christmas too much to wait to put up a tree, so we put up two."

Pulling his gaze away from her, Deckard quickly glanced down at the sheet and then asked, "Day two: make ornaments?"

"My mom is super crafty. She would come up with some design for us and we'd make an ornament to place on the garland she draped on their fireplace mantle."

"I'm guessing the previous year's ornaments are placed on the tree?"

"Always." I smile, remembering my mother's delicate touch as she treated each ornament as if it were her most prized treasure. "She had a special spot for each and every one."

January's smile grew in fondness until it dawned on her again that there was no Christmas, and she'd never again see the look of delight in her mom's eyes.

"Okay, you also have written down: make gingerbread houses and cookies, family night with a Christmas movie -"

She interrupted, adding, "It was going to be my turn this year."

She clarified what she meant when he looked over at her in confusion. "We took turns every year to decide who got to pick the Christmas movie the family would watch. It was my turn this year."

Setting the notebook down, he gazed at her in complete rapture. "Really? What would you have picked to watch?"

"I don't know. I hadn't really thought about it."

"If you had to pick right now, what would have been your choice?"

January thought about it. There weren't many Christmas-themed movies that she loved or cared to watch more than once. Last time she chose *White Christmas* because she knew it was her mother's favorite.

"Um, I always had a soft spot for Tim Allen in The Santa Clause. It's probably the only Christmas movie I've seen a few times and I don't hate it."

"I bet it's great."

Deckard paused, appearing to wait for January to come to some sort of conclusion, but she wasn't sure what that was supposed to be. His steady gaze on her had January squirming in her seat with nerves. What about this man had her feeling like a teenager sitting with her first crush?

"Continue," she motioned for him to keep reading the list.

"A Christmas parade. Where was the parade?"

"Here in town, it's probably similar to the celebration. But the town really loved it. All of the clubs and businesses made floats and went up the streets for the twelve blocks of downtown. It was great. And there were little booths with hot chocolate and cookies. Everyone was always smiling and we all sat together on the sidewalk edges in the center of town."

"That sounds nice. We don't have a parade, but I imagine it wouldn't be hard to convince the town to do one."

"How would you decorate the floats? Isn't solstice mostly symbolized with stars and snowflakes?"

"Yeah. I guess there wouldn't be much variety. But you never know." He shrugged his shoulders with a smile on his lips, then looked down to continue reading through the list. "Christmas Eve dinner and gift exchange.

"Imagine Thanksgiving in December and a birthday to the extreme."

She bit back a laugh as Deckard's eyes widened at her description. The two events were the closest thing she could think of to describe Christmas.

"No way."

"Yes. People would go all out for Christmas presents. Kids would write lists of gifts they wanted from Santa at the North Pole, and if they were on the nice list, they'd get some of them, or all if you were lucky enough."

"What if you were bad?"

"Oh, if you were on the naughty list, you got coal. At least, that's always been the tale. I was always on the nice list."

"I find that hard to imagine."

"Really," she says coyly, taking a sip from her water.

"Oh yeah. You have sinner written all over you."

January's eyes cast down at his assumption. She wasn't a sinner, but she'd gladly get down on her knees and start confessing to him.

Deckard paused and let his words sink and settle in her mind.

"I. ..uh. . .don't know what you mean."

"By the way we kissed last night. I'm certain that you do."

"Oh," she sat mollified at his answer. She absolutely wanted a repeat from last night with him. And at the way her core tightened just imagining the kiss again, her body was on par for a repeat performance. Maybe she was a sinner after all.

Her mind started thinking about tugging him into the supply closet of the bakery and finishing what they had started last night.

A slam brought her back into the moment and she found Deckard had closed the notebook with a bang on the table.

"Let's do it."

Her cheeks heated, wondering if he somehow knew what she had imagined just seconds ago.

Bashfully January ran a finger along the edge of the table as she asked, "Do what?"

He shook his head, some of the dark wavy strands falling into his eyes. "Your list. Let's do it."

She immediately paused her movements. "What?"

"I don't think I'll understand what we're missing unless I experience it. I mean, this list and your descriptions are too detailed to be a coincidence, and I told you that I believed you. I want to know all about how you celebrated Christmas. I bet your friend Samantha would want to join in too. Though I'm man enough to admit it, she may be tiny, but she scares me."

Chuckling, January piped in, "Don't worry, she scares me most days too."

Deckard reached across the table and took her free hand into one of his. "So, what do you think? Show me your Christmas."

"I feel like that could be a terrible euphemism for something sexual, but yes, I'll show you my Christmas."

Chapter Four

ogether they left the small bistro and walked back toward Nick's Knacks General Store. January had worried about not calling out of work, but when she got a hold of Samantha, her friend informed her that their boss wasn't even in the office.

She also invited herself to join them as they searched for a tree – no questions asked, even after January gave her a brief rundown on the missing holiday. She would be meeting them in thirty minutes.

Inside the store, January wasn't prepared for what she saw. Though she knew there was little chance that there would be anything related to Christmas, she still held out a glimmer of hope. But as they walked farther into the space, her heart dropped. She imagined it looked like it would any other time of the year. The shelves were stocked with all the items a small town would need in the winter: snow scrapers and shovels, de-icer, boots, and snow gear.

Deflated, January followed Deckard around the shop, pointing out the items they needed to chop down the perfect tree. He grabbed an ax, a tarp, and a large bucket to fill with dirt to hold the tree. She made the mistake of asking if they sold a tree stand and he looked at her as if she had grown two heads. She hadn't considered that there wouldn't be any available. But she was not going to be deterred.

On their way out the door, she noticed the sale on Halloween décor. A white and black string light set caught her attention in the large bin.

"These are perfect. Do you happen to have any ribbon?" she asked enthusiastically. She wondered if this was how her mother felt every year when it was time to decorate their tree.

Deckard pointed her toward an aisle with craft supplies and she eagerly skipped down the aisle, sighing in relief when she found a three-inch wide red ribbon. She grabbed a few spools of it and also some thinner white satin ribbon for the ornaments they could make.

At the checkout counter, she found Deckard standing handsomely at the register and she piled her findings in front of him. January noticed that he had added some gloves to their pile as he rang them out.

"So, where is a good place to look for a tree?" Deckard asked just as Samantha bounced over to them.

"The woods, of course!" the woman shouted as she grabbed the bags from the counter and rushed back out the door as quickly as she came.

"I guess we're following her?" Deckard joked as he pressed his hand to January's back to guide her out of the store. They shared a knowing smirk at Samantha's quick entry and exit.

"Seems that way. I hope you brought a GPS because she will probably get us lost."

Holding up his phone to signify that he had the GPS covered, Deckard laughed as he stopped in front of his pickup truck. January didn't want him to know how much she admired the vehicle with its black-as-night paint and large tires, but she was certain as he took in her smile that he knew anyway.

She clapped her hands gleefully as he held the door open for her to climb in. They were going out on an adventure today and January had a hard time hiding her excitement. With her foot on the running board, she heaved herself inside the cab, settling against the luxurious leather of the seat. At this height, Deckard was only slightly below her eye level, and as he moved to close the door, she gripped the collar of his jacket, leaned in, and kissed him the way she had wanted to in the bakery.

She had thought that their first kiss last night had made her head spin because it had been a lustful moment in a public place, but as her lips brushed against his now, she knew it was more than a one-time thing. They had chemistry, neither of them could deny that, but there was something more that she couldn't put her finger on. January had been burned so badly by her last relationship that she was skittish to try another. It seemed there was another magic at play, and instead of fighting against it as she had two days ago, January was going to revel in it.

His tongue peeked out and swiped against her lips, begging for entrance, and she greedily accepted his plea. Strong arms wrapped around her waist as Deckard stepped between her legs. Like last night, January felt like she couldn't get close enough to him. It wasn't just the clothes or the place. She felt their connection was only held together by a small tether slipping away with every second that passed.

"I can't get enough of you," Deckard murmured against her mouth before he greedily dove back in to take more. January moaned lustfully at his assault.

January almost bit Deckard's plump lip when a car's horn honked beside them, startling them both. With her hands still clutching the lapels of his coat, as Deckard jumped back in alarm, he almost pulled January along with him.

"Let's go, people. We're on a mission!" Samantha shouted from behind the wheel of her compact car.

Deckard closed the door, then shuffled around the truck's hood before sliding inside.

The truck pulled out onto the street and Samantha quickly steered her vehicle in line behind them.

"You know, I'm surprised at how easily Samantha came on board with this entire Christmas thing. We both know that I believe you, but most people would think you needed to be committed. No offense."

"That's the thing about Samantha, her friends are her family, and if I told her that there was a twelve-foot abominable snowman living in my backyard, she wouldn't question me at all."

"You mean you don't have one?" he feigned shock and January slapped his arm with the back of her hand.

"Seriously. Samantha knows when I'm lying, she always has. And she's always up for a reason to add sparkles to her world."

Deckard nodded as they reached the town limits and turned on the radio. January hated to admit that it seemed strange to hear regular music playing on the station. He must have caught her expression.

"Why the sullen face?"

"Are there no winter solstice songs?"

"No, I don't think so. What has you looking like you just lost your cat?"

"Christmas music was kind of like nails on a chalkboard to me. They took over all my favorite stations and you couldn't go anywhere without hearing them. But now that they aren't around, I kind of miss them. I know that sounds silly." She shrugged her shoulders, knowing there was nothing she could do about the missing music.

"No, it doesn't. It seems like maybe you took the holiday for granted."

"It wasn't just me, everyone seemed to, but I'm the only one that had a countdown for it to be over."

"I'm sorry, January. Maybe you could sing one for me?" He looked at her with large puppy dog eyes and blinked those incredibly long eyelashes that men seemed to always be graced with

She laughed loudly at his suggestion, so hard, in fact, that she clutched her stomach as the chuckles soared out of her.

"You absolutely do not want to hear me sing. You've never heard a more horrific sound."

"I seriously doubt that. I bet you have a great voice, low and sultry."

January had never sung in front of anyone and no one had ever asked. Her brother had once heard her singing in the bathroom when she was eight. She had been getting ready for a party, and when she stepped out of the room, he had told her she sounded like a dying animal. January hadn't sung since that day. Now that she had time to ponder the situation, maybe her brother was just being mean and not honest.

"There is one song that I kind of always liked."

"I'd like to hear it. Please." Deckard looked over to her and smiled. Puppy dog eyes were long gone. And there was no way she could deny him anything when he smiled at her that way. Heck, he could ask her to dance naked outside and she wouldn't think twice about it.

Closing her eyes, January began to hum the beat of the song. It came as second nature, having heard it every year since she could remember. Then the lyrics started to surge as she sang, "Have Yourself a Merry Little Christmas."

The truck stopped, but January kept singing, the words flowing through her without abandon. She felt the tears pooling in the corner of her eyes until it became too much and one lone tear escaped, sliding down her cheek.

As the last word poured from her lips, she felt Deckard's hand touch her cheek to wipe away her sadness. January was embarrassed by her reaction to the song, but it was too late to make excuses. Her eyes opened and she took in the tree-lined landscape before them.

"Look at me," Deckard demanded in quiet confidence. Her head turned toward him, but she couldn't bring her eyes to meet his. "Look at me, beautiful." January heard the sadness flitting through his gravelly voice and she drew her eyes up to meet his. He said with a sullen smile, "I'm sorry. I didn't realize how hard that may have been for you."

January tried to toss aside her sudden sadness, shaking her head, replacing it with a small smile. "I'm fine. Honestly. I think it just got to me that I'll never get to hear the song again."

Deckard opened his mouth, appearing like he wanted to say more, but a knock on January's window brought their attention to Samantha, waiting anxiously outside, rocking back and forth in her designer boots.

The handle felt cold under her hand as January reached to open the door, but she stopped when she felt Deckard's grip on her arm.

"Hey, I know that this may be your last Christmas, but we're going to make it the best one. Trust me."

And she did. She knew that he felt the same undeniable pull toward her that she felt toward him, despite knowing each other for a couple of days. Sometimes you just knew right off the bat that you could trust someone. She felt that way about Deckard.

"Okay," she whispered as he released her arm and silently commanded that she stay in her seat.

His profile looked so strong and masculine as he passed the front of the vehicle and January couldn't believe that he was unattached. Except, she didn't really know that. Just assumed. He had a woman waiting for him back home in Atlanta for all she knew.

She didn't have a chance to ponder his singleness because Deckard opened the door to the truck and lifted her out of the seat, kissing her forehead as he set her on her feet.

As he stepped toward the truck's bed to grab the supplies, January's eyelids squeezed together until just the smallest of slits remained. The fresh powder that had fallen from the night before acted like a mirror as the sun shone down on it, practically blinding anyone looking directly at the ground.

Automatically her hand reached up to hang over her eyes as she waited for them to adjust to the light, but she was saved when Samantha held out her hand with another pair of sunglasses.

January gladly took them from her friend. "Thanks."

Sliding the frames onto her face, January immediately felt relief from the bright sun. She wondered if Deckard had a pair in his truck,and as he approached, she noticed he was wearing a pair of Wayfarers.

She licked her lips as she took him in. He had removed his coat and January watched him strut toward her and Samantha in a dark red sweater pulled taut against his chest and arms. His dark jeans looked like they were made to fit perfectly around his muscled thighs. Even the gray scarf he kept tossed around his neck only added to his sex appeal.

January was a goner. She didn't even feel the chill in the air as she watched him take each step closer.

"Wipe away the drool," Samantha whispered and January shushed her. "Not that I blame you. Because, damn," her friend added.

Deckard held the ax and bag across one of his shoulders while his other arm came up and wrapped around January.

"Ready?" he asked them both.

Just as January began to take a step, Samantha reached out and held her back. "Deckard, why don't you go ahead and we'll be right behind you? We need to catch up."

At January's look of horror, Deckard began to laugh. "Sure. Just don't dawdle too long."

The women watched as he walked away, whistling an unfamiliar tune as he went. January was sure both of them were staring at Deckard's backside with every step he took.

"Girl, you are one lucky woman. That man is delicious."

"He really is. I don't even know why I said no to him in the first place."

Her comment broke both of them free from their butt-induced trance, and Samantha looked up at her. "You were scared of getting hurt again. I get it."

"I'm going to get hurt again, but I'll be prepared this time."

"Maybe he'll surprise you."

January was hoping that maybe she could convince him to stay and not go back home to Atlanta, but she knew he had a business to run. He had mentioned while they were searching through articles that morning that he had applied for a loan to open his own practice. It was what he had always wanted to do. But, she surmised, she could enjoy Deckard while he was in town.

As they began to walk, Samantha asked, "So tell me how all of this happened?"

"With Christmas?"

"No, you told me about the wish and ornament on the phone. And it totally seems plausible, knowing you. But what I want to know are the juicy details leading up to all of it. Like, how are you and Deckard together at all?"

January smiled as they began walking and she gave her friend a rundown on the past two days. She loved Samantha's reaction when she mentioned answering the door to Deckard in just a shirt and flashing the man her panties when she fell. And both women had to fan their faces when she described their kiss after dinner.

"Man, I'm just going to live vicariously through you. Grayson is great, but we've never had anything heated like that."

"But you guys just started dating," January claimed and Samantha pinned her with a steely gaze that she could sense through the sunglasses both women were wearing. "Okay, I get your point," she added, realizing that she and Deckard had just started dating as well. But it didn't feel like it. Whatever they had was something more potent than any year-long relationship she'd ever been in.

Silence followed as they kept a step a few yards behind Deckard until he came to a stop and turned toward them. They were standing in a beautiful clearing in the middle of the forest. It was something out of a fairytale.

"So, how do we do this?"

January realized that she hadn't taken the time to describe to either of them what her perfect Christmas tree would look like. Eastern White Pine surrounded them on all sides, which would make the perfect tree. Now, she just had to find one that was the right height and width.

"We need a tree around seven and a half feet tall, and full. We also need to run our hands across the branches to check and see how healthy the tree is. We don't want a lot of needles shedding."

The group split up but stayed close as they each focused on the mission at hand. To January, every one seemed too tall or too bare. She couldn't find *the one*.

"Hey!" Deckard shouted five minutes later from across the clearing. "What about this one?"

January rushed toward the sound of his voice and stopped when she caught a glimpse of the tree standing proudly beside Deckard, who looked equally as proud. His chest was puffed out and he rested his hands on his hips. It was adorable.

"That's perfect," she whispered. The emotions the moment conjured up soared through her so quickly that she almost fell to the ground in her haste to get to Deckard. January launched herself into his arms, wrapping her legs around his waist at the same time. She was glad he had sat down his ax because he was able to enfold her in his embrace.

"It's so perfect." January felt her breath move against the skin of his neck as she murmured.

"All right, Paul Bunyan. Let's get this show on the road. I can't feel my toes," Samantha jokingly complained.

Deckard allowed January to slide down his body, adding a squeeze of her hand as he stepped away to grab the ax. With his guidance, the women stepped out of the way and watched as he chopped down the tree effortlessly.

In the plastic bag, Deckard retrieved and unpacked a tarp and some rope, creating a makeshift sleigh to carry the tree back to the truck.

He refused their assistance to pull the contraption up the hill, but he didn't seem to struggle with the weight, only adjusting his gloved hands once. The trees fell behind them until they were a small line in the distance and the two vehicles were in view.

"Do you want to come over to the house and help decorate?" January asked Samantha, but her friend politely declined as she had special plans to play out a mountain man fantasy with her beau.

They hugged goodbye just as Deckard finished loading the tree in the back of his truck.

"Ready?" she asked him as he closed the gate.

"Yep. Let's get out of the cold. Up you go," he gestured as he moved to hold her door open.

The ride to her house was quick, and though she knew that Deckard had been in her space before, she nervously fidgeted in her seat, twisting her fingers and picking at the seam of her jeans.

He must have noticed because his hand settled on top of hers after he turned off the truck.

"Hey, what has you so worked up?"

He moved her hands so that he could grasp the one closest to him, intertwining their fingers. Instantly she was soothed by his touch. It was a revelation to January that this man could calm her down on the spot.

"I have no idea."

"Is it me coming inside your house? I've been here before."

"Uninvited, I might add."

Chuckling, Deckard said, "But always welcome." She joined him with a giggle and her nerves dissipated even more.

"Do you want me to help bring the tree inside?"

"If you can open the door, I think I can manage."

They both slipped out of the truck and January rushed up the stairs of her porch to open the door for Deckard, who had already lifted the tree and tarp free from the truck. Then she remembered the bucket and dirt they had picked up at the general store. Skipping back down to the vehicle, she grabbed the supplies and situated them in the house where her mother had placed the Christmas tree every year.

Together Deckard and January positioned the tree in the large metal bucket and settled the soil around it, making sure to add some water when they were finished.

Standing back to gaze at the flourishing addition, she noticed Deckard had a contemplative expression with pinched lips and narrowed eyes.

"What?"

"It's nothing, but what if there are bugs?"

It wasn't what she had expected to hear, but now that the notion was out there, January was doing her best to keep from freaking out.

"Um. . ."

Breaking his façade Deckard laughed heartily, bending over with his chuckles. Once he seemed to calm down, he said, "I shook it outside and dusted it with powder we keep at the shop for plants brought indoors. I'm sorry. You should have seen your face."

Cocky bastard.

"Yes, well, you should see your face."

January pretended to have her feelings hurt, crossing her arms against her chest and pouting her lips.

"Aw, don't be upset with me," Deckard pleaded as he reached out and pulled her closer. Even her stubbornness was no match for him.

"I'm not," she admitted with her body pressed against him. She could feel the steady beat of his heart against the palms of her hands as they rested on his chest.

Something in the air shifted and neither January nor Deckard seemed to be able to pull away from each other. There was an invisible force drawing them closer. Deckard's strong hand moved up her arm until it rested on her cheek. January resisted closing her eyes and relaxing into his touch even though every fiber of her body told her to do just that.

"You do something to me. I've never met anyone like you before. You're a complete surprise," he whispered, his gaze never faltering.

She wanted to tell him that she felt the same, that he completely flipped her world on its axis, but the words didn't come. January was too lost in the blue of his eyes as they stared back at her.

But it seemed that Deckard didn't need to hear a reply. He simply bent his body forward until he could capture her lips with his. This kiss wasn't soft and sweet.

Instead, it was a continuation of their kiss in the forest. It was fueled with passion and need, and January knew that if she let it continue as fervently as it was, they'd soon progress to another level that she wasn't sure either of them was ready for. At least not mentally. Physically her body was cheering on the sidelines with pom-poms waving joyously in the air.

Deckard's hands trailed beneath her coat and silently urged her to discard it. She quickly shrugged it from her shoulders and it pooled on the floor at her boot-clad feet along with Deckard's scarf that January slipped from around his neck.

They couldn't seem to keep their hands off of each other. Shivers quaked across January's body when she felt his fingertips linger just under the hem of her sweater above the waistband of her jeans.

"Deckard." The name escaped her before she could rein it in. It was said in need, desire, and every ounce of lust in her body. He answered her call without words but by sliding his hand across her skin to her stomach, where his fingertips lingered on the button of her jeans, silently asking for permission.

January nibbled on his lip, giving him the answer they both were seeking, but just as the button flicked free from the loop, January's cell phone rang in her purse. And she recognized the ringtone she wouldn't be able to ignore. Both she and Deckard moaned in unison at the intrusion.

"Sorry, it's my mom," January quickly apologized as she took a step back and began rifling through her bag on the small table, searching for her phone.

"Where are you?" her mother shouted on the other end of the call just as January answered.

"What?" glancing around the room, she tried to ignore the tent in Deckard's pants. A few seconds passed before she remembered what she had been looking for. The calendar in the corner had a bright red circle over today's date. Even with Christmas not in the picture, her mother expected her to be at their house for Augustus' arrival.

"Shit," she murmured in panic.

"Language," her mother scolded. "Can I expect you soon, January?"

"Yes, I'm on my way. Time got away from me, that's all. See you soon, Mom."

Ending the call, January ran her hand through her hair in exasperation. She was enjoying her time with Deckard and really hated to lose a moment with him, but she knew that neither of them was ready for him to meet her parents. And as she looked over, she could see the disappointment oozing from him and understanding. He was close to his family and knew that there would be no backing out.

"I'm sorry. Can we postpone until tomorrow? We can decorate and make some ornaments at the same time."

"Yeah, sure." The letdown was evident in the tone of his voice. It was low and sullen, not his normally deep voice laced with sex. "I should probably go help my grandparents anyway."

"I'll even make dinner tomorrow."

"It's a date," he said as he leaned down to pick up his scarf and her coat.

As he handed her jacket over, January felt a new distance between them. And she really disliked it. "Deckard, I wanted to thank you for today. For, well, everything really and for believing me." She could see that she was breaking through that steely wall he was erecting.

Leaning down to press a kiss on her forehead, the same spot he had left a peck earlier, Deckard said, "You're welcome. I'll see you tomorrow. Text me when you want me to come over."

"Okay."

Snow had started to fall, and January watched from the picture window situated at the front of her house as Deckard backed his truck out of her driveway. It was silly to miss him already, but she did. She craved more time with him. More than the few hours they'd had so far.

With a heavy sigh, she slid her jacket back on, grabbed her purse, then headed out to her car, locking her front door behind her.

January wasn't sure how she would make it through the night without feeling the guilt weighing heavily on her. Not just the remorse of having to send Deckard away, but the responsibility for the reason Christmas was no longer in existence would be her burden to bear for years to come.

RENEE HARLESS

Chapter Five

Enjoyment at a family get-together around the holidays was uncommon for January. So, she was surprised at how much fun she had spent the previous evening with her family. The arrival of her brother made January want to appear put out that she had to suspend her plans, but as her nieces swirled around her legs when January stepped through the door, her chilled exterior thawed. Even Scrooge herself had a hard time staying angry when the cutest princesses wanted her attention.

She barely thought about Deckard the entire time she was there until her mom brought up that one of the neighbors had seen them outside the general store yesterday in a compromising position.

Her parents wanted to meet him even after she explained that Deckard wasn't sticking around and had no intention of doing so. Her mother huffed and scooped up the kids to make some clay stars for the solstice display on the mantle of their fireplace. Her father, on the other hand, had told her that she was worth sticking around for. January wasn't sure how true that statement was or if it was just her father letting her down gently, but it felt good just the same.

It was no surprise she had disappointed her mother again when she clarified that she would not be attending the solstice festival with them. January had considered messaging Deckard and asking if he could come back over and continue what they had begun earlier when she arrived home later that evening. But she didn't want to become that needy woman.

Raising her arms above her head January stretched, then she sat her bag on the coffee table, taking a good look at the empty Christmas tree. It was a disappointing sight.

Her phone rang as she was getting ready for bed and fear shot through her when her mother's name flashed across the screen. In a rare moment that January would remember for the rest of her days, her mother had called to apologize for how she acted about the festival. Her mother was also concerned about how January had acted. "Out of sorts," her mother had claimed. With a deep breath, January let it all flow. The wish, Christmas, the guilt, all of it. And her mother listened. She didn't judge. She didn't scoff. She simply opened her mind to the possibilities.

It was the first night in a long time that January went to bed without dreading the following day.

In the morning, January was surprised to wake to a message on her phone from Deckard sent around 1 a.m., wishing that he had come back over when she got home. As she rolled over in bed she smiled to herself, but her grin didn't last long as her phone rang, flashing a number from her office across the screen, reminding her that she had a day at the office to look forward to.

The only plus side to a busy day at work was that time usually flew by and this day was no exception. The fact that it was Friday helped motivate January even more.

It was a relief to be back home with the weekend in full force. January tossed her bag onto the small entry table as she entered her house and immediately walked toward her bedroom, shedding her clothes with every step. The turtleneck went after the shoes, then her bra was removed with a flip of her wrist against her back, and finally, she shimmied her pants down as she approached the bathroom. January wanted to take a long hot shower before Deckard arrived, but she knew she didn't have the time. He was on his way over and

January still had to come up with something to make for dinner.

Even though she knew she needed to rush through the shower, she couldn't control herself from gliding her hands down her soapy skin as she imagined how the night alone with Deckard may go.

Her fingers slipped between her legs and swirled effortlessly around her clit, sending shockwaves through her body. She pictured Deckard in her mind. Her hands were his hands. Her touch was his touch. The building orgasm was caused by him, not her, and it was delectable. January heard her cries echo against the tiles of her shower stall and she had to brace herself against the glass door with her free hand as the quakes purged through her body.

It took a few minutes, but January finally came back into herself and stared blankly at the knob of the shower as the steam rolled around her. Begrudgingly, she reached out and twisted the knob to turn off the water with her limp limbs. She stepped out of the stall, grabbed her towel from the hook, and wrapped it around her body.

Though the towel was made of the softest cloth, it felt rough and scraped painfully against her sensitive skin. A curse mumbled from deep in her throat as she twisted the towel into itself to secure it around her body just as her doorbell sounded.

She shouted, "Coming," but knew that the person on the other side of her door wasn't going to hear.

Tucking her body behind the door as she opened it, she was surprised to see Deckard standing there with Chinese takeout dangling in a bag from his fingers.

"You're early," she exclaimed.

In response, Deckard held up his bag. "I come bearing gifts."

January rolled her eyes as she ushered him inside, ignoring his growing grin as he took in her towel-clad body.

"You can set that up in the kitchen and I'll slip on some clothes."

"Don't change on account of me," he pointed out, earning himself a growl from January.

"Behave. I'll be right back."

On her way back to her bedroom, January picked up the clothing she had strewn about the room and hallway in her haste for a shower. She carried the pile, dumped it in her hamper, and then pondered for a moment about what to wear that evening. Obviously, she wanted to look cute, but she also wanted to be comfortable.

In her closet, she sifted through the slacks, blouses, and dresses, but none of them seemed to fit what she was looking for. Comfort overruled fashion as she opened her dresser, pulling out a pair of black leggings and an oversized sweatshirt she had cut the neck out of so that it hung over one of her bare shoulders.

Her hair was still twisted up on top of her head to keep it from getting wet during her shower and she decided to leave it there.

The scent of Chinese food wafted into her room and January decided what she was wearing would have to do because her stomach was making noises she had never heard before.

As she stepped into the kitchen, she had every intention of telling Deckard how good the meal smelled, but she was struck dumb as she found him piling some of the food onto plates, looking like a domesticated god.

"Wow," she mumbled, taking him in. Today he wore a light blue shirt, almost the same color as his eyes, and she swore that it would be her new favorite color. It looked amazing against his tanned skin and the scruff of his chin.

"You going to stand there all day?" he asked without raising his head or eyes in her direction. He knew she was there all along. "Or do you plan to join me?"

Deciding not to try to cover up her ogling, January strolled into the kitchen and planted herself on one of the bar stools at the island. "I'm starving. I could smell this all the way back in my room."

"I asked Samantha which meal was your favorite, so you can blame her if you don't like it. But if you do, just forget I said anything."

January giggled as he set the plate in front of her, then walked around to take his own seat.

"Don't worry. I'm not picky. There isn't a Chinese dish I dislike. So you're in luck."

"I knew there was a reason why I liked you."

They ate their meal in silence, the comfort of each other's presence enough to keep their minds at ease.

Last night January had started thinking of the different kinds of decorations and ornaments her mother used to have them make for their tree. A few stuck out clearly and she was lucky enough to find the supplies in town during her lunch break. The string and bags of popcorn were sitting on the counter while the air-dry clay and plastic balls were in a basket in her living room.

She had a plan and hoped that Deckard was on board.

"I like you like this," she heard above the noise of her slurps from the lo-mein noodles she held on her fork.

With an unattractive number of noodles still dangling from her mouth January turned to look at Deckard in confusion. "Like this?" She was fairly certain that she looked like a pig at the moment and that she most likely had soy sauce splattered on her face. A neat eater she was not.

Deckard laughed as he grabbed one of the eggrolls sitting on a plate on the counter between them. "No, like this." He motioned up and down to her outfit. "Relaxed. Carefree."

"I am far from carefree or relaxed. Being around you has me on high alert."

"Well, it shouldn't because I think that you're just as beautiful like this as you are all done up. Hell, I even like you in just a ratty T-shirt. Actually, I won't lie. I prefer you that way the most."

"You just like my legs," she joked as she added a new forkful of noodles into her mouth.

"I do, but it's more than that. I really just like you. You intrigue me."

She pondered that for a moment. Besides their attraction, she didn't know much about him except that he was a dentist. She knew she should probably remedy that soon, but January was afraid that she would get more attached to him the more she knew.

"Do you think we should try to get to know each other better or just leave things as they are?"

A clatter rang out as Deckard dropped his fork on his plate and turned ninety degrees on his stool to face her direction. When she followed suit and set her own fork on her plate, Deckard grabbed her knees and twisted her to face him, placing both of her legs between his. She loved the feel of his hands on her thighs.

"What do you want to know?" he asked.

"Like your favorite color. Where do you like to vacation? Are you a homebody or do you like to go out? I don't know. It's silly."

The feeling of warmth spread through her as Deckard settled his hands on her knees. "Why is it silly?"

"Because we're like a week away," she explained.

Cocking his head to the side, he analyzed her as he asked, "A week away from what?"

Agitation pulsed through her at his response. "Until you leave!"

Nodding, Deckard didn't look as freaked out as she felt. She was already falling for this man that has made himself at home in her life, and she wanted to blame someone for how she was feeling, but January knew that she was the only one that could control her emotions. She stole another glance toward Deckard and found him smiling as if he had just watched a kid perform a magic trick.

"Did you forget that you're leaving? Did you need a reminder?"

"No, I didn't forget. I just wanted to focus on spending my limited time with you. And we could always figure out a long-distance thing if we wanted."

"I don't think I'm cut out for that. I'm too needy."

Leaning toward her, the air around them started to crackle as invisible sparks ignited between them. Deckard's hands began to slide up her inner thighs as he brushed his cheek against hers.

"I know exactly what you need," he whispered in her ear and January's body shivered at the feeling of his breath sweeping across her neck.

"What's that?"

A trail of delicate kisses lined her neck and led up to the corner of her mouth, where Deckard placed a final kiss. "You need. . .to show me how you want this tree decorated so that we can move on to getting to know each other better."

Playfully she slapped his shoulder as he stood from the stool and gathered their plates.

"You know that was mean, right?"

"The anticipation will be worth it. Now explain to me what I'm going to do with string, popcorn, and a needle," he said as he held up the unpopped popcorn bag and the spool of string.

Three baking sheets held the clay creations Deckard and January had created two hours later. Most were shaped using cookie cutters January had in her kitchen, while a few were shaped like snowmen and stockings. Deckard had been surprisingly good at molding the clay with his fingers. January would bet her favorite pair of shoes that Deckard could mold her body just as easily.

They had also grabbed some pine cones from out in her backyard, tying some string to them so they could hang on the tree.

January watched and held back her laughter as Deckard attempted to unravel the Halloween-themed lights and drape them on the tree. She would have thought Deckard would be able to tackle the project in a calm manner, but she saw that he was getting frustrated. There was a reason why she preferred pre-lit trees. January wasn't patient enough to untangle lights.

She offered to help him, but he shrugged her off. His determination was evident. January went back to her task of creating the popcorn garland. Unfortunately, just as much popcorn made it into her mouth as it did on the thin string.

"All done!" Deckard shouted as he stood next to the tree with his hands on his hips just above the low-slung denim.

"Good. Me too," she said as she grabbed the garland coiled on the table. "Can you help me wrap it around the tree?"

"Of course."

Together they draped the garland and ribbons she had picked up at the general store around the tree. They wove them in and out of the branches as they worked their way from the top to the bottom.

When they finished, January plugged in the lights and then stood back to admire their work.

"Wow," they murmured in unison. Deckard moved from his spot next to the tree to stand beside her, wrapping his arm around her waist.

"This really is something," he murmured in her ear.

It was. The tree was fun and bright, but as January scanned it over, she realized something was missing.

"We need a tree topper."

Gazing down at her, Deckard asked, "What's that?"

"Usually, it's an angel or star, sometimes a bow. Essentially, it's like the cherry on top."

"I see. Do you have anything like that lying around?"

January contemplated. She wasn't sure what she had around the house, but she was certain she had something that would work."

Her stare traveled around the room, but nothing caught her eye until she landed on the large marquee D made of metal that sat stoically on her end table. He caught her eye as the idea formed.

With the help of her guest, she placed the letter on the tree and was amazed at the transformation.

"It's beautiful," she stated softly as she stared at the tree.

Deckard's voice had changed a few octaves lower when he replied, "Yes, it is."

Instinctively she looked up at the man that had moved next to her and met his pinned stare.

"Deckard." The name flew from her mouth in a voice she didn't recognize. It was wanton, needy, and a far cry from how she usually sounded. Deckard not only had her feeling emotions and desires she had never felt before, but he even had her sounding different.

January didn't know how to ask for what she wanted.

Where was Santa when she needed him?

"If you keep looking at me like that, I won't be held responsible for my actions," Deckard growled. The bellowing noise had January's panties soaked before he could even finish his sentence.

"How am I looking at you?"

"Like you wish I'd strip you bare and have my way with you. Does that sound about right?" Deckard asked, extending his hand to run down her arm. At the contact, January jumped. She was so lost in his words and how they made her want to liquefy into a puddle that she didn't notice him move. The conscious effort to blink was a summon she could barely retain, let alone focus on what Deckard was doing.

His fingers skimmed across the naked skin of her shoulder where her sweatshirt had dipped. The move was both innocent and seductive, causing goosebumps to rise all over her body. Despite the room's warmth, the hairs on her arms stood up on their ends as she watched Deckard lean his head closer to her exposed skin.

An invisible circular path was drawn as Deckard moved his fingers aimlessly around her bare shoulder. "I really like this spot on you." His lips placed the softest of kisses along her collarbone. "I like how you react."

Something in the back of her mind registered that they had only known each other for a couple of days, regardless of how her heart told her that it didn't matter what her brain was trying to say.

But she couldn't stop blurting the words, "Are we moving too fast?"

He immediately paused, his full lips hovering over her skin, and January wished that she could turn back time just a few seconds, especially when Deckard straightened his stance.

"Is that what you think? I won't push you, January. We don't have to do anything you're not ready for."

A tiny sigh flew from her lips. "I have no idea what I want. I just know that regardless of how hard I fought it at first, I want you."

"Why did you fight it?" he asked as he tucked a wayward strand of hair that had escaped from her ponytail behind her ear.

"I don't know. I was scared, I think. I've never had relationships go very well when the holidays are involved and well. . .you were like the epitome of holiday cheer when we met."

"I was?" he asked, January forgetting that though they met the same way, the situation was different.

"You were busy decorating a ton of Christmas trees and helped me find an ornament for my parent's tree."

Deckard took a step toward her, even though she didn't know they could be any closer. The hand drawing lazily on her shoulder moved to cup her jaw. "Did I help you find what you were looking for?"

The way he asked the question, January wasn't sure if he was speaking about the ornament or something else entirely. She licked her lips, the sudden dryness of her mouth making it difficult to answer. His eyes scanned her face, those blue eyes of his darkening to an almost black. Reflections of the lights on the tree glittered in his irises.

She painstakingly swallowed the lump lodged in her throat. "Yes, you did," she whispered, wishing she hadn't spoken and ruined their moment seconds ago.

She wanted to tell him that it wasn't just the ornament that he had chosen for her and the beautiful inscription. It was that he gave her a chance to be with him. She wanted to reply with, "You," but somehow she didn't think he'd understand the depth and feeling of the reply.

"I guess I should probably head out because I know that if I stay any longer, I'm liable to try to convince you to let me have my way with you."

"That would probably be a good idea. I think I just need to wrap my head around everything. And also make a mental note that you have a little alpha in you. I didn't see that coming."

"I'm full of things that would surprise you," he added just as he leaned forward and pressed a kiss to her cheek. "Gingerbread houses tomorrow?"

With the reminder, January instantly perked up. "Yes! And after talking with my parents last night, they want to join in. So, you . . .um. . . get to meet my parents."

His hand slid down her arm until their fingers latched together. "I'm looking forward to it." With a gentle squeeze of her hand, he pulled away, taking heavy steps toward her door. "Goodnight, January."

"'Night, Deckard."

As he stepped outside, January grabbed a blanket from her couch and draped it over her shoulders, shielding her body from the cold as she moved out onto the porch behind him. His massive figure disappeared behind his truck and she watched as the vehicle's lights turned on and then slipped away into the darkness as he drove away.

The night closed in around her, and her consequences weighed heavy on her shoulders. One wish changed everything and January didn't know how to come to terms with her feelings about it. She just knew that the wish didn't alter the fact that her parents were still focused on a winter holiday that overshadowed her birthday and that Deckard wasn't going to stick around. There was no way a dentist with a flourishing career would upend his life to move to Pineville, Ohio, with a population of a few thousand.

It was quiet as silent snow fell around her porch. January took it all in. She wondered if she'd miss Christmas next year or if she would continue to celebrate it despite her mistake. She just didn't know.

Looking up at the sky, a break opened between the clouds filling the black canvas with stars and an idyllic crescent moon.

"Oh, what a mess I've made," she whispered to the open air as she leaned against the porch railing. "It seems silly to make a wish in hopes that it all returns to how it was. I'm not even sure it would be possible. Heck, I don't know how any of this is possible." January shook her head in exasperation. Focusing on the brightest star amidst the darkness, January sighed deeply, the crisp air stinging her lungs with the inhale. "I wish that there was a way to fix this."

Just as she finished her wish, the remarkable sight of a shooting star soaring high in the sky caught her attention.

"Very funny. I already made a wish on a snowflake. I'm not about to make a wish on a star."

Remembering the day ahead, January went back inside her house and started making a list of the ingredients she would need for the gingerbread houses. Her cupboards weren't stocked with what she needed. It looked like a run by the market in the morning was in order.

But as she lay in bed softly snuggling with her duvet, January was worried that she'd wake and everything would be changed again.

"That's what you get for making silly wishes," she murmured an hour later just as her eyes finally grew heavy.

RENEE HARLESS

Chapter Six

It was when she walked past her third booth selling solstice displays, January knew she had made a mistake. Everywhere she looked, groups gathered around discussing the next day's celebration at the Pineville Winter Solstice Festival.

All January wanted to do was grab the fresh items she needed and make her way back home, but that didn't seem like it would happen. She had no less than twelve different people already stop her to chat and ask if she was going to be at the festival, which she had absolutely no idea about.

Just when January was about to give up, she spied the back of someone she was getting to know all too well. Deckard stood at a booth holding a green bag in one of his hands while the other was hanging loosely at his side.

But what caught her eye was the beautiful woman speaking with him animatedly. There was a familiar air around them. Whatever she was telling him had Deckard's rapt attention. January couldn't even deny that the first emotion that flitted through her veins was jealousy. It was callous and naive, but she felt it nonetheless. And though January knew that she had no claim on Deckard, she had hoped that they were on the same page.

The couple was only a few feet away, but Deckard hadn't turned around to spot her yet. She spun on her heels and decided she would rather stop by the grocery store instead of having fresh ingredients than face one more second of Deckard and this woman together.

"January!" Her name was shouted above the crowd and January's attention turned to her best friend waving and pushing through the crowd. From the corner of her eye, she saw Deckard turn around. He had a deer caught in the headlights expression, as if he never imagined finding January there.

"Hi, Samantha," January said, faking cheerfulness as Samantha made it to where she stood.

"I didn't expect you to be here. Celebrating isn't really your thing."

"Yeah, it's not. I came for some fresh ingredients, but I seem to be out of luck," January pointed out as she held up her extensive shopping list and empty hands.

"Well, I wouldn't quite say that." Samantha grinned coyly as she nodded her head in Deckard's direction. Even without Samantha's not-so-subtle gesture, she could feel Deckard's eyes on her as he approached.

"I would. He was looking very familiar with the beautiful blonde over there," January hissed, hating the sound of jealousy spewing from her.

"Oh, her -" Samantha began but was interrupted by Deckard as he came to a stop beside January. "Hello, ladies."

They both replied in greeting and then an awkward silence fell around them until it was too much for Samantha.

"Well, I was just going to see if you wanted to get lunch, but I am certain you two have plans." Her friend scooted away eagerly, which January wished she could do as well. "Call me later!" Samantha yelled over the crowd as she disappeared back into the masses.

January didn't know what had overcome her, but instead of turning around to look at Deckard, she made the childish decision to walk away.

"Hey! January." Unfortunately, her plan was thwarted as Deckard took a few long strides to catch up with her. "What's going on with you?" he asked. January knew that as a man, Deckard had no idea what he had done wrong or that he had asked the wrong kind of question.

"What's going on with me?" she sneered, feeling virtual fangs lengthen down from her canines as if she was readying for attack.

"Whoa, whoa. I have no idea what caused you to act like this, but please take a second to calm down."

January stared at him as if he had grown two heads. Two ugly sinister heads with green ooze and warts. Luckily for Deckard the mystery woman that was causing the green-eyed monster to free herself from January's subconscious joined their meeting, making them a trio.

"Deckard," the woman purred with her sultry voice and even January couldn't hide the shivers it created. "Is this the woman you were telling me about?" January's eyes immediately narrowed at the man that had barged into her life while she waited for his reply.

To January's horror, Deckard wrapped his arm around the woman and smiled down at her before looking back at January with that smirk that had previously brought her to her knees. She was regretting every moment she let him hold her close.

"Yes, it is, Whitney. This is January. January, this is -"

"Nope." January butted into the conversation with a hand saucily placed on her hip. "I'm leaving. I'm sure your. . .friend, Whitney, can explain it to you. Thanks for wasting my time."

With her back turned and the crowd filling in the space between them, January barely made out the sound of Deckard asking his far-too-beautiful companion what he had done wrong. She passed a hot chocolate stand, wishing she had the time to stop and grab a cup of the frothy goodness, but in her anger, January stomped by without a backward glance – until she ran smack dab into a wall of muscle.

"Oomph," she groaned as she rubbed the tip of her nose to ease it from the pain of the muscled mass collision.

"January." Deckard's voice was a strange mix of urgency and terror that put January on high alert. She had never heard anyone sound so anguished before and it made her look up and pause.

"January, I swear I didn't do whatever you think I was doing. Whitney is my dental hygienist," at January's uncontrollable growl, Deckard added, "And my cousin."

Hollowly, January replied, "Your cousin?"

"Yes, cousins. Whitney and I grew up together. We're more like siblings. She came to see our grandparents for the solstice."

Completely embarrassed, January turned her body and face away from Deckard as she aimed her attention toward the gravel beneath her feet. She didn't know what to do. Apologize, for sure, but she hadn't done something on this level since high school. Groveling didn't come naturally to January

"Deckard, I. . ." She was speechless. There wasn't an apology big enough to encompass the jealousy she had felt and how she had lashed out at him – grouping him into all of her past boyfriends.

"Hey, I get it," he reached out and gripped her hand with his free one. "I didn't know she was coming in town this weekend or I would have mentioned it."

Holding up her hand, January explained, "No. No, it's not okay. I shouldn't have assumed what I did."

"I can't blame you. I would have done the same for someone I cared about."

"I'm sorry, Deckard. I'm just going to head to the store and finish my shopping." January fumbled through her words, trying to back out of this conversation as gracefully as possible.

"No way. What do you have on that list? I can help you grab some things."

"Shouldn't you spend time with your family?" Deckard lightly grabbed her elbow and steered her toward the back corner of the marketplace.

"Nah, I see them enough and we'll be with them tomorrow, remember? I'd rather spend more time with you." He smiled down at her and January felt herself swoon with each step.

They reached the first destination and grabbed jarred spices from her ingredient list. "So, I'm sorry that I assumed the worst."

"Stop, January."

His command halted her and she looked up at the handsome man holding a root of ginger in his hand.

"I just feel bad, that's all."

"I know, and I get it. So stop apologizing. Now, let's get your ingredients. I'm ready to try these gingerbread houses."

With a small smile, January lifted another ginger root and reached for a jar of cloves. "Make, not eat."

"Wait, we don't get to eat them? What kind of establishment are you running?" In feigned horror, Deckard's eyes widened and his mouth hung agape, which only caused January to giggle.

"You eat them on Christmas day. Or at least that's what we did. But we can also make some gingerbread cookies and decorate those."

"See, I knew you'd come up with something for me and my stomach. I'm a growing boy." He patted his flat stomach and January wished she could slip her hand under his sweater and feel the taut muscles beneath because she knew without a doubt that Deckard didn't have an ounce of fat on his delectable body.

Deckard's lips graced the edge of her ear as he leaned toward her. "Your cheeks are turning pink. What are you thinking about?"

Immediately she quipped, "Nothing."

"Little liar. Don't worry. I'll get it out of you later."

In silence, they finished loading her bag with molasses, brown sugar, and the spices they had already collected. One of the stands displayed candies that both January and Deckard's mouths salivated over.

"I bet you're ready to punish me right now for all this sugar, aren't you, Doctor?" January teased as she flung one of the sugar-coated gummy balls into her mouth.

"If you were my patient, I would scold you for more than your sugar intake. But it's okay to let yourself indulge in something delectable every now and then." January wasn't positive, but she had a sneaking suspicion that Deckard was referring to more than just the candies presented to them. He only added to her confusion as he grabbed a handful of chocolate candies and shoved them into his mouth.

She expected when he smiled that his mouth would ooze with chocolate froth. But not Deckard – she should have known better. When he smiled, his perfectly straight white teeth glistened as if they weren't holding back a mound of goodness behind them.

The woman selling the candies handed January a cup of coffee that she had ordered.

"I hate you sometimes, you know?"

"Why?" he asked as he reached for her cup of coffee to take a sip. Usually, January didn't like to share her beverages, but she figured since she wanted to do intimate things with Deckard, they could probably share a drink.

"Because you're like. . .perfect. You look like a freaking dark-haired Thor, you're obviously smart, and you can make me laugh – which is a hard feat in itself. Believe me. That makes you the perfect catch. Why do you even want to hang out with me?"

As he handed her back the cup of coffee, Deckard asked, "Why wouldn't I want to hang out with you? You're beautiful, and smart, and I like making you laugh – it may be my favorite sound. And, January, you should know that I want to do much more than just hang out with you."

She felt the foam slip from her fingers, but she could do little to stop it as the cup tilted back and spilled the hot liquid all down her favorite ivory blouse. She instantly pulled her ruined silk shirt away from her chest, wishing that she had kept her jacket closed instead of leaving it unzipped.

Deckard rushed to help her, but the damage was done. "January, are you okay?"

"Yeah, I'm just a clumsy mess."

Deckard grabbed her bag and tossed the coffee cup into the trashcan nearby, ushering her away from the growing crowd around them, watching in rapt interest. "Come on, let's get you out of that shirt before you catch a cold."

"Can't catch a cold from a wet shirt in the winter," she added smartly as she followed his brisk steps toward the parking lot.

"No, but you can catch hypothermia," he replied in a voice that sounded both concerned and angry. His stance was stiff as he rushed them through the crowd. His steps were quick and powerful.

Finally, they reached her car and he immediately reached into her purse to grab her keys, unlocked her doors, and started her car. She imagined that he was turning the heat on full blast.

"Get in and take off your shirt." Deckard didn't just ask; he commanded.

"Excuse me?" she asked in horror.

"You need to get out of the wet shirt and we need to see if you have any burns. Take it off and zip up your coat. I'll make sure no one is looking."

"Yes. . .well. . .you're looking."

One of his dark brows raised in defiance and January knew it would be a battle she would lose if she fought against his demand.

"Fine," she growled, stomping over to where he stood by her open driver's side door. January glared up at him, boldly slipped her arms out of her coat, and handed it over to Deckard. Without moving her gaze away from his eyes, she quickly maneuvered every button of her blouse, yanking it free of her jeans with an earnest tug, and then pulled it free of her body with ease she didn't feel.

January didn't care if anyone saw her, it was not like she was naked, but as a brisk wind picked up while she was standing in her bra, her nipples puckered behind the confines of the nude lace from the chill. She could see that Deckard was doing his best not to look down at her chest, attempting to be the gentleman he was, but his perseverance was wearing thin.

He held out a shaking hand with her coat when she asked, "I don't think I have any burns. May I have my jacket, please?"

Even though January knew that he was trying to keep her from getting sick, she felt a small sense of pride that she was able to affect him in a similar way that he affected her.

Jacket in place, she zipped the material completely, the top of the coat reaching just under her nose. "Better?" she asked, the sound muffled by the shield.

"Not even close," Deckard replied as he tugged down the zipper a tad so that he could see the remainder of her face. "There, now I can see you. Go get warm. I'll be right behind you." He placed a kiss on her lips but gave her little time to react as he spun around on his heels and headed toward his own vehicle.

She hoped that he remembered her parents were going to join them tonight to help make the gingerbread houses because with the way he had just left her, he had a completely different itinerary on his mind.

~

The kitchen was a mess. Counters and cabinets were covered in dough and sugar due to an unfortunate incident between Deckard and her hand mixer. But they had been laughing so hard the entire time she almost forgot to grab the baking sheet from the oven in time.

Together they cut out the individual patterns for the sides and roofs of the houses and placed all the different candies and decorations in bowls. Deckard's eyes widened in delight as January brought out a new set of ingredients from her fridge.

"What else are we making?" he asked adorably with flour smeared across his cheek. She touched his face to wipe it away, but her hand lingered there for a beat longer than was necessary.

"Sorry, you have something right here," she tried to explain, but her voice was soft and breathy. January felt the air around them shift. Her body began to feel warm all over. Deckard extended an arm and rested his hand on her hip, his fist gathering the material of her red sweater in its grasp.

January's thumb stroked back and forth just above the scruff on his cheek as his thumb did the same on the exposed skin of her hip. They didn't speak, but January could feel the anticipation building until the barrier between them shattered.

With a yank, he pulled her toward him at the same time she had begun to slide her hand toward the back of his head. Their kiss was hot, frantic, and uncontrollable. Neither fought for dominance. Their mouths and tongues brushed and licked with familiarity.

Deckard moved them so that January's back pressed against the island and she felt the bulge in his jeans press against her stomach. She yearned to feel it between her legs.

She didn't have to wait long.

Using his muscled arms, Deckard lifted her effortlessly onto the island counter, neither caring about the mess they were making as they pushed the ingredients aside. Leftover flour now coated her pants and his hands. With his arms on either side of her legs, he caged her in and stepped between her legs. His impressive length settled against her center. January moaned uncontrollably as Deckard rocked his hips against her.

January knew that she had gone a long while without an orgasm, but she never imagined that the friction from Deckard's jean-covered erection would bring her to her release so quickly.

"Oh, fuck," she said as her muscles began to tense. But then Deckard took a step back, leaving her in all of her aching glory.

"What are you -"

"You're not going to come unless it's my hand, mouth, or cock in that pussy."

He began to grip the edges of her sweater and lift it up her body, but January was too lost in his words. Damn, it was like adding pure oxygen to an already stifling fire. January wasn't sure if she could explode from a sentence alone, but she was pretty freaking close.

"You teased me earlier. I want a better look," he added as he tossed her sweater off in the distance. "Damn, you are perfection."

January couldn't think, couldn't speak. She could barely remember to breathe as Deckard unhooked her bra and used his large hands to cup her breasts. They felt like ice against her heated skin and her back arched at the sensation, her nipples pebbling beneath his palms.

For some reason, January didn't second guess their actions as she had yesterday. This moment felt different. It felt right.

He must have known that she was getting lost in her own head again because he leaned forward and captured one of her breasts in his mouth. January had to slam her hands against the counter to brace herself against the onslaught.

It was a heady sensation overtaking January's body that she had very little conscious thought about the things going on around her. All she knew was that she wanted Deckard's shirt gone. She blindly reached out and gripped the back of his shirt, tugging with very little strength to slide it over his head.

Deckard seemed to realize her desire because he pulled away to lift the shirt from his body. January found herself groaning as she pried her eyes open to look. He was tanned and muscled to faultlessness with a small smattering of hair across his chest. A soft trail of hair led from his navel to the cock still nestled within his jeans, and January couldn't look away, but Deckard took the choice away from her.

With a quick flip, the button on her jeans came undone and Deckard expertly slid down the zipper plunging his hand under her lace panties. Her moans echoed in the kitchen at the intrusion of his fingers skimming across her clit, seeking out her core.

"Deckard." She ached for him, yearned for more than just his touch, and Deckard somehow read her mind as he slipped two of his fingers deep within her tight sheath. "Oh my god," she mumbled incoherently.

January couldn't hold back as her second climax approached with his deft fingers. One of her arms swung out and clawed at his back as she rode his hand to her release.

"Let go, baby," he whispered against her neck and January tried to chase her release over the edge, but she couldn't get there. Her muscles and legs were so tight, waiting for the sensation to take over, but she just couldn't get there.

Deckard heard her mewling plea and leaned forward, sealing her lips with his. That's all it took. A split second of time where she was lost in him and not her own head. She bit his bottom lip as she fell apart, feeling the twinge of metallic flavor swirl in her mouth.

He held her up as her muscles loosened, one of his arms braced against the counter while the other wrapped around her waist. It took January a few minutes to drift back into herself. The smell of gingerbread filtered through her senses and she remembered where she was.

Sitting up straighter, her eyes immediately fell on the bulge, still thick and solid, beneath his jeans. Wanting to do something for him, she dropped down from the counter and skimmed her hands up his legs as she knelt before him.

But he didn't let her get very far as his hands slipped under her arms and lifted her back onto her feet.

"What are you -" she began, but he cut her off with a kiss.

"As much as I would enjoy seeing your mouth on my cock, this was about you, not me. You can thank me later." He winked. He freaking winked and January almost melted into a puddle at his feet.

Deckard glided his hand across her shoulder as he brushed her hair away from her face. "I enjoy you like this."

"What? Naked from the waist up?" she joked, but Deckard only lifted the corner of his mouth a smidgen.

"No, I mean relaxed and sated like this."

"Oh."

He continued to trail his hand back and forth along her naked back. Normally she would feel exposed and attempt to cover up her bare breasts. Instead, January felt a sense of freedom. But the reality of where they were and their plans went off like a buzzer in the back of her mind.

"I should probably put my clothes back on," she sighed as she looked around the kitchen for her bra and sweater.

Deckard reached for his shirt and pulled it over his head, covering up all the beauty that w

as his chest and abs. She still couldn't locate any of her items, though. Deckard must have spotted one piece because he reached into the leftover batter bowl and pulled out her bra, now covered in brown sugar and molasses.

He held it out to her, the strap dangling from his fingertip. "Sorry," he said sheepishly, his chin tucked down as he shrugged his shoulders.

"That's okay. Let me go grab another. Can you look for my sweater?" January walked away to her bedroom to search for another bra leaving Deckard with the task.

New bra in place, she continued to replay their kitchen exchange in her head as she reappeared out of the hallway. So engrossed in her thoughts, January never heard her front door open or heard her parents speaking with Deckard – who was trying to toss her the sweater frantically.

But it was too late. Her mother and father turned just as she tried to back away into the shadows of the hallway. A knowing smile grew on her mother's face while her dad turned an angry red face toward Deckard, who quickly shuffled toward her with the sweater in hand. Without her assistance, he pulled the garment over her head and tugged it over her body, capturing her earring in the loose fabric.

"Ow!"

Deckard stopped his frenzied movements at her cry and let her finish dressing. "Sorry," he mouthed, referring to both catching her earring and her parent's arrival.

Pulling herself together, January attempted to act as if nothing was amiss. "Mom, Dad, this is Deckard, my. . ."

"Boyfriend," he added as he held a hand to her parents. "It's great to meet you finally."

January didn't want to admit how nice it was to hear Deckard call himself her boyfriend.

She watched her father squeeze Deckard's hand, trying to intimidate the poor guy, but Deckard adjusted his hold and pressed right back. Her mother looked at the men admonishingly and then turned to January and asked, "So, what about these gingerbread houses you were telling me about."

"I still need to make the icing, but first, let me show you my Christmas tree."

Her mother gleefully clapped when January flipped on the lights and delicately touched each handmade ornament. But instead of feeling content with the joy she was giving her mother, the guilt that January had been battling came back in full force.

She left her parents at the kitchen table as they assembled their gingerbread house while she went to work making another batch of royal icing for the other two houses.

"Hey. Still upset about the no shirt thing?" Deckard asked as he sidled up next to her, placing his hand over hers to stop her maniacal stirring of the icing mix.

"No," she scoffed. "I'm over that." Her whisk began slamming against the edge of the glass bowl as she thought harder about the damage she had caused with that stupid wish.

Deckard gripped the edges of the bowl and pulled it away, causing her to look up at him in confusion. "Then what has you so worked up?" Reaching out, he gripped the whisk from her as well and set all of it aside so that their attention wasn't interrupted.

"I'm just feeling guilty, that's all. My mom loved the Christmas tree, as I knew that she would. I stole that joy from her. It's my fault, Deckard." She shamelessly turned her attention to the flecks in her granite countertop, not wanting to see Deckard's face as the realization of her mistake would finally hit him.

Something cold touched her cheek and January's head jerked up in an instant to find Deckard standing even closer to her with icing dripping from his fingers.

"What the?" she asked as he swiped more icing down her nose. "Are you serious right now?"

"Stop thinking about the wish," he said, and when she opened her mouth to argue, Deckard attempted to run his sticky fingers across her other cheek, but she ducked and spun away before he could reach her. January neared the bowl and stuck her own fingers in the gooey mess, collecting a blob and reaching for Deckard's face. Except due to his height, she was at a severe disadvantage.

Instead, he captured her wrist and brought her fingers to his mouth, sucking the fingertips between his lips as he licked away the icing. She tried desperately to ignore her growing desire for him as he swirled his tongue around her fingers, but the sensation was overwhelming. January tried to pull her hand away, but Deckard's hold didn't relent.

Her free hand reached out to grip the counter, but she failed when she came in contact with the bowl of icing. Coating her other hand with the concoction, January used Deckard's hunched stance to her advantage and ran her hand from the top of his head down and across his cheek, covering his hair and half of his face in the icing.

He immediately released his hold and looked at her in surprise.

"Did you really?" She tried not to laugh at his look of complete shock, but a giggle slipped free. "You're going to pay for that," he said as he reached for the bowl, but she beat him to it and held it against her body as she took a step back and then another. But he followed until soon they were both running through her house, dodging furniture and laughing hysterically at the same time. January barely remembered that her parents were sitting at the kitchen table. When she caught her mother's eye, January watched as a knowing grin spread across her lips and then turned her attention back to the completed gingerbread house on the table.

January had slowed enough that Deckard could finally grab the bowl from her grip and capture it in his own. He scooped an overzealous amount onto his hand and hovered it in the air as he devilishly grinned down at her.

"Deckard, don't," she warned as she took a step back, her hands held in the air in surrender.

"You got icing in my hair. That means war."

"I'm sorry, I'll even help you clean it out," January placated.

Shrewdly, Deckard stalked toward her, his hand still floating above the bowl with dollops of icing dripping from his hand until he had her back pressed against the refrigerator door. He leaned forward and January closed her eyes, anticipating the chill of the icing skidding across her face, but all she felt was the gentle brush of lips against her nose.

Her eyes flashed open and she looked up at Deckard in confusion.

"I accept your apology," he said as he carried the bowl and his hand over to the sink. "We can make another batch of icing, but I need to get it out of my hair first."

Filled with relief January joined him at the sink. Using a dishtowel to drape over his shoulders, she had him lean over the basin as she used her faucet to clean the gunk from his hair. He moaned as her nails scraped across his scalp in a gentle massage.

When she was done cleaning the white icing from his dark strands, she turned the faucet off and took a step back to grab a clean dishtowel from an island drawer to dry his hair with. But as she returned with the towel in her hand, she was met with a sprinkling of water against her face.

Deckard had stood up and flipped his hair away from his forehead, which caused the loose droplets to land on her. It appeared that he was about to stage war number two.

With the towel in hand, she remembered how her father used to twist the material and flick it toward someone, resulting in a smack of whatever body part the end of the cloth landed. It was always in jest, but she recalled how the tip of the material would sting like hell.

January twisted the cloth in her hands, grabbing two ends of the rag, creating a line of swirls. Then with a flick of her wrist, she let the towel go on one end, expecting it to land against Deckard's hip. But she should have known better. That man knew what she was thinking before she even did most of the time.

His reaction was better than she could have ever imagined as he caught the loose end of the towel and tugged her toward him. She smiled sheepishly as she landed against his body, expecting him to retaliate against her assault, but he did nothing more than sink his free hand into her hair, tilt her head back, and crush his lips against hers. She was lost instantly. Her fingers lost their grip on the rag as she trailed her hands up his chest and around his neck, clasping her hands together behind his head. He drank her in, swallowed down every ounce of fear and guilt left in her body and set her free.

A cough sounded, breaking them apart. January found her father looking back and forth between the two of them.

"Where is your house?" her father asked, referring to the gingerbread house. January tried her hardest to come up with a believable excuse, not that it would matter; her parents had been in the same room the entire time.

Luckily, Deckard chimed in, "That batch got a bit overmixed."

"Yeah," she added. "We need to make a new batch."

Her dad looked like he wanted to say something more as he pinned his eyes to Deckard's arm still wrapped around January's waist, but her mother saved them all.

"How about your dad and I go into the living room and order a pizza for dinner?"

Grateful for the suggestion, January said, "That sounds great, Mom. Thanks."

She watched her parents walk hand-in-hand to the living room, leaving January and Deckard alone in the kitchen.

"You know what this means?" Deckard asked and January looked up at him in confusion. His one-sided grin caused her hackles to rise.

"No, what?"

With a forceful tug, he again turned her in his arms and brushed his lips against hers. She liked that he always wanted to hold her close. "Now we're alone."

It wasn't long before they were lost in each other again. January never expected to connect with someone so quickly, but with Deckard, she couldn't imagine being with anyone else. Time ceased to exist when they were together. Gravity held no power because she was floating on cloud nine high above the stratosphere just by being in his presence. But she had to remind herself that this was not the way it should have been. The guilt was what was going to drag her through Hell until she could figure out a way to make it up to everyone. Not just to her mother and family for denying them their love of the holiday, but even Deckard's smile wasn't as bright as it had been when he was pointing out the different ornaments on the Christmas trees in his grandparents' shop.

And she knew that none of them would ever understand the burden that she felt. All she could do was show them what she had denied them and hope they didn't hate her for it.

She hated herself enough for all of them.

RENEE HARLESS

Chapter Seven

The previous night had been fun with her parents and Deckard. Unlike most events with her family, January didn't feel overshadowed by her siblings and their amazing achievements. Not even her parents grilling Deckard about his life and job made January feel any less significant. Of course, how could anyone fault a man that was a doctor and looked as dreamy as Deckard did?

Her mother was smitten with him after he explained how he was helping his grandparents during the solstice season at their shop. Her dad fell for the man when Deckard offered to help remove a fallen tree from her parent's backyard. As if she hadn't already felt like she was falling head over heels for him, her parents had to approve of him too. It was only going to make it much more difficult when he left on the twenty-fifth.

She had ushered both Deckard and her parents from her house after they finished the pizza, much to Deckard's surprise. But she was struggling to come to terms with how she was feeling and what she knew would happen when he left. January needed space and time to decide if she would risk the hurt.

When she woke the following morning, she texted Deckard and declined his invitation to spend the solstice celebration with him and his family. He continued to message her after the initial declination, but January was too embarrassed to answer. She ended up spending the morning in bed feeling sorry for herself.

Lying in bed reading a book seemed like an excellent way to keep her mind off her new boyfriend and how she was being a complete bitch to him at the moment, but of course, the book she was finishing up from a year ago was an epic romance that left her crying at the end of the story.

She had thought about taking a long bath or wrapping herself in a layer of blankets and settling in a chair on her back porch to watch the snow fall, but neither of those seemed appealing. She was depressed about the fact that she was falling in love with a man that was going to leave. January thought that maybe she could do something to get him to stay, but there wasn't much that she, or Pineville, could offer him. Her heart set her up for failure.

This feeling was slaying her and she felt she had no say in how her future would turn out. But January knew better; she had changed her own future. She had changed it for everyone.

Lazily, she finally made her way from the bed to the couch, where she snuggled under a heavy blanket and turned on a channel of sweet romance movies, determined not to leave that spot through the afternoon and evening.

So thoroughly engrossed in a scene playing on the screen, she almost missed the knock on the door, but when the door opened without her assistance, January knew she had no reason to worry. Only one person would barge into her house unannounced – Samantha.

"Get up," her friend declared as she ripped the blanket off January's sweat-suit-clad body.

Trying in vain to capture the blanket from Samantha, January shouted, "What are you doing?"

"Trying to get you out of your funk."

"I'm not in a funk," January huffed as she sat up on the couch and crossed her arms against her chest in defiance.

Her friend balled up the blanket and took a seat next to her. "Look, I get that you're freaked out with how fast things are moving between you and Deckard -"

"How did you. .?"

"He texted and said you bailed on him today. It wasn't hard to figure out that a relationship, in general, scares you. And then the fact that he might not stay here in Pineville is just throwing your emotions out of whack.

"And to top it all off, your world has been completely flipped upside down. For us, nothing has changed, but for you, nothing is the same."

"How can I fix it?" January asked.

With a heavy sigh, her friend said, "You can't. All you can do is move forward. Let's celebrate the Christmas you remember, and then when it's all over, you move on with your life as if nothing was amiss."

"Keep moving forward."

"That's right; because the past is the past and we can't change it. But we can look toward the future."

"The past is the past," January murmured to herself, mimicking Samantha's wise words. She had spent so many years living with her hands grasping at the hurt of her childhood that she let the past mask the wonderful things of the present and future.

"Now, while I'm all for some movie nights at home, this is not one of those times. Go get showered and get dressed in something warm."

With a grunt and a push, Samantha not so gracefully shoved January off the couch.

When she almost dropped to the floor, January shouted, "Hey!"

Ignoring her, Samantha made herself comfortable in January's spot on the couch. "Go, you have ten minutes."

"Why? Where are we going?" January asked as she made her way down the hallway, shuffling her sock-covered feet the entire way.

"Doesn't matter. Just dress warmly."

January worried that Samantha was going to drag her to the Pineville Solstice Celebration Festival downtown tonight through her entire shower. As she pulled on her jeans and knee-high boots, she even considered making up an excuse to keep from going out. But she knew Samantha wasn't going to fall for any of it. When her friend was determined to do something, there was no backing out of it.

Of course, January felt she owed it to Samantha after the sound piece of advice she had given her not too long ago.

"Keep the past in the past," January reminded herself as she shook her hair free of its twist, letting it fall in soft waves around her shoulders. January looked over herself through her reflection, loving how the blood-red sweater set off her peach skin tone and the blonde highlights in her hair.

Satisfied with her appearance, she went to her coat closet and grabbed an ivory scarf and hat. While she had sat on the couch, she noticed how heavily the snow had begun to fall. It was surprising to have Samantha venture out to her house with the storm the way it was, but in Pineville, everyone knew how to maneuver in the slushy mess.

"Samantha!" she called out. "Can you give me a hint about where we're going? Am I dressed okay?" Too busy expertly knotting the scarf around her neck, January walked into the living room and looked up in alarm when she didn't receive an answer.

She had expected to find Samantha playing on her phone, ignoring the world around her. January didn't expect to find Deckard standing beside her Christmas tree, holding her coat in his hand.

"What? How?" she stuttered as she tried to figure out why Deckard would be standing in her kitchen looking so devilishly handsome when he should be with his family.

"I want to take you somewhere," Deckard softly said as he held open her coat for her to slip into.

"Deckard, I'm sorry, I. . ." she tried to explain but couldn't quite get past the lump in her throat. January hadn't ever heard Deckard sound this way. He was almost. . .sad. And her first thought was that she upset him by ditching him and his family today, and now he was returning to Atlanta early.

Served her right, she thought.

The assurance she was waiting and hoping for didn't come, but the soft squeeze of Deckard's hand in hers as he guided her from her house was more than she could have asked for.

January knew better than to ask where they were going. For all she knew, he was going to drag her to his grandparents' house just to spite her. Silently he helped her into his truck and backed out of her driveway, heading away from town.

January wouldn't blame him.

The silence was beginning to crush her as the world darkened around them. Their surroundings changed from homes and sidewalk-lined streets to fields and trees.

It was all too much.

"I'm sorry for bailing today. I'm just feeling a bit overwhelmed and guilty, and I think it got the best of me. I didn't mean to upset your family."

She wanted a reply, needed one to ease her consciousness, but Deckard took the hand resting on the center console and gently clasped hers.

"Don't you have something to say? Anything? Like, are you mad? I can't read you right now and it's freaking me out."

The truck effortlessly maneuvered around a bend in the road, then Deckard stole a quick glance at her, grinning warmly, but he still remained silent.

Her agitation was starting to rise and January wanted nothing more than to lash out at Deckard, but in the back of her mind, she felt that maybe she deserved his reservations. She was the one to back out of their plans.

The beautiful blue glow from the moon illuminated on the profile of his face and January felt an ache ping in her chest. She was going to miss him, this beautiful and stubborn man that didn't give up when she rejected him the first time, this man that undoubtedly believed her tale of wishing away Christmas, this man that wanted nothing more than to spend what little time he had in Pineville with her.

She couldn't take it anymore and with a final plea, January's voice cracked. "Deckard, please."

"We're here," he revealed as he put the truck in park and cut the engine. January turned to look out the window and found a beautiful barn illuminated by outdoor Edison lights. Horses were standing in their stalls, their heads peeking out through the doorway.

"What's this?" she turned back to ask him, but Deckard was already jumping down from the vehicle, his reply a slamming of his door. His pace was quick as he trudged around the truck and opened her door, holding out a hand to help her down.

"Before you say anything, I already had this planned out, but when you bailed this morning, I had to call in reinforcements," he explained as he escorted her toward the barn that looked like something from a Christmas card.

Someone had taken the time to shovel a path from the entrance on the road up to the barn. January was grateful since the snow had continuously fallen for the last three days creating almost a foot of snow on the ground.

"Samantha," she whispered. She squeezed his hand to get his attention and waited for Deckard to turn his face toward her before she continued. "Deckard, I really am sorry. I was just not thinking straight."

He stopped walking and used their conjoined hands to pull her closer. She could feel the heat radiating off his body, even in the chilled temperature. "I know and I get it. I won't lie and say I wasn't upset you canceled this morning, but I understood."

"So, you're not mad?"

He didn't answer with words. Instead, he leaned forward and kissed her. It was a perfect kiss. Not just because the snow softly fell around them and the idyllic red barn with string lights casting them both in a dim light, but she and Deckard had unparalleled chemistry.

A cough sounded from close by and January found herself jumping back almost falling into the bank of snow had Deckard's strong arms not reached out and gripped her waist.

"Sorry. Mr. Spruce, I have everything ready for you," the young worker said as he bashfully brushed his hands against dirt-covered pants.

"Thank you, Thomas. Is your father ready for us?"

"He sure is, sir."

January watched as the teen scampered away toward the barn, but Deckard brought her attention back to him. "You ready?" His growing excitement was palpable.

They started walking again in the direction of the barn as she added, "You still haven't told me what we're doing yet."

January waited for him to spill the secret, but as they approached the top of the hill, she didn't need to wait any longer. A beautiful white stallion stood proudly with a large wooden sleigh trailing behind him. A bundled-up man sat along the front seat with the horse's reins in his hands.

Deckard had planned a romantic sleigh ride with her. And she almost ruined it. Her feet glued themselves to the ground as she took it all in.

As if her guilt wasn't weighing her down already.

"Stop. I can see the wheels turning. I wanted to do something special for you. It may not be Christmassy, but this is one of my grandparents' favorite things to do during the winter solstice. I wanted to share that with you."

"Am I dreaming right now?" she asked, her eyes never leaving the vision before her. "Deckard, this is. . ." she trailed off, unsure of the exact words she could use to describe this moment.

Deckard offered for her. "Beautiful. Perfect. Something the best boyfriend in the world would do?"

Finally, her eyes pulled away from the sleigh and she looked at Deckard in all of his smug glory. Rising on her tiptoes, January placed a kiss on his scruff-covered cheek.

"It's all of those things. Thank you, Deckard."

"You're welcome, beautiful."

He helped her step into the sleigh and then followed behind, covering them both with the blanket provided by the driver. January marveled at how much the trip through the snowy field calmed her. It could be the noise of the horse clopping along the path or the whoosh of the sleigh being pulled. January thought that it had more to do with the sound of Deckard's steady heartbeat as it pounded beneath her ear where she rested her head against his chest, or it could be the up and down movement of his chest with each breath that he took. Whichever reason, January was lulled into a sense of serenity she had never felt before.

Tilting her head to look up at Deckard, she marveled at how this man, who had been a stranger only a few days ago, had come to feel like such a part of her. She would miss him when he was gone, but she was forever changed because of him, and that meant that a piece of Deckard would always be with her. She realized that it was going to have to be enough.

"Thank you," she said, loving how he looked down at her and smiled before pulling her tighter against him.

This was heaven, and she didn't want it to end. But just like Christmas, they were on a deadline.

The sleigh ride lasted an hour, and they were headed back toward her house. The drive seemed shorter than before, but January wondered if that was due to anticipation. She wasn't going to keep Deckard at arm's length when they reached her home. She was planning on succumbing to the cravings she had been fighting against.

She was a strong, independent woman; if she wanted to have sex with a man she'd known for less than a week, then she could. January felt that she had a stronger connection with Deckard than with any of her previous boyfriends or lovers, which meant more to her than time.

Just like he had at the barn, Deckard stopped the truck and put it in park, except this time, he didn't cut the engine. Instead, he turned to look at her. She wanted to squirm in her seat; she was nervous and how he looked at her made her body heat. The combination churned her stomach.

"Do you want to come inside?" she whispered. She sent a silent prayer to the heavens that Deckard could understand her because she could barely understand her own voice.

The blue eyes across from her glistened from the light beaming from the dashboard and January tried to search them for an answer but came up empty.

"Are you asking because you think that's what I want, or is it what you want?"

Great question, she thought.

But she knew her answer and didn't have to ponder for longer than a couple of seconds. "I would really like for you to join me tonight, Deckard. All night." She hoped that he understood her message, and if he didn't, then she really needed to work on her flirting skills.

She watched in rapt awareness as his hand lifted away from the steering wheel and slipped under her chin, caressing her jawline. Deckard's thumb brushed against her bottom lip, and it took every ounce of strength she possessed to keep from licking at the appendage. Her stomach clenched as she thought of all the amazing things he could do with that thumb and his hands.

"I'd love nothing better than to come inside with you."

She must have misheard him because she swore he said to come inside her, but she shook her head to rid herself of those thoughts even though they sounded right up her alley.

As they walked up toward her porch, neither spoke or noticed that the lights in her house and on her porch had been turned on. Deckard halted her immediately as they made their way up to the top step, begging her to give him the key to her house. She floundered as she tried to open her purse.

Somehow, Deckard grabbed the key from her bag and unlocked the door, opening her to a kitchen and living room filled in all its Christmas glory. It was beautiful and classic and January could barely contain herself.

"Wow," she murmured as she looked around. String lights lined her kitchen and living room, and the porch was covered in garland and more string lights.

"January."

"When did you do this?"

"I didn't. I was with you, remember?" A soft touch cupped her chin in hopes of pulling her attention away from the decorations. Deckard added, "If people truly love something or someone, they never forget. It stays with them for their entire life. Maybe your parents were so easy to accept the idea of Christmas because they still felt their love for the holiday somewhere deep inside. They did this while we were gone with Samantha's help."

Tears completely blanketed her eyes, threatening to spill over the corners. She hadn't ever considered how much people loved the holiday. She only knew about the hate she had felt. Hate that seemed so silly in retrospect. Sharing all the things she remembered about Christmas, things that she had done with her family, made her realize that her hate had always been misplaced. Maybe it wasn't hate that she felt toward Christmas. It was just timing and bad luck that seemed to follow her. And, well, her name. January knew there wasn't much she could do about that without breaking her parents' hearts.

Taking a deep breath, January let the smell of wintergreen and pine fill her lungs. A hint of cinnamon also lingered in the air and she knew that this was a smell she would always remember. Not just of the wintery cold season, but of Christmas. With her head tilted back and eyes closed, she took another inhale. Deckard's hand had moved from her cheek to her neck and she loved the way his thumb drew lazy circles along her pulse point.

Slowly opening her eyes, she straightened herself, peered over Deckard's shoulder, then giggled at what she found behind him. Not a sprig, but a bushel of mistletoe hung in the hallway about a foot away from where they were standing.

"I think my mom is trying to send us a message."

Pointing toward the greenery, Deckard followed the extension of her arm and chuckled as he turned back toward her.

"Luckily, the reasoning for hanging mistletoe hasn't changed. Or I'm assuming it hasn't."

In the dim lights of the house, Deckard walked backward, pulling January with him, until they were situated just beneath the mistletoe. She waited for the kiss, thinking he would immediately pounce and kiss her senseless, but she should know by now that Deckard wasn't like everyone else.

The knit hat she wore was delicately lifted from her head and tossed aimlessly into the living room. Next, her scarf and coat followed the same path. The way Deckard carefully removed each item felt more intimate than any time she had laid with a lover. A sensual moan drifted between her lips when Deckard's fingers dove into her hair and started combing through the waves pointing in all different directions from the static.

January was enjoying the sporadic massage so much that she closed her eyes and let herself focus on the feel of his hands. But then his hands stilled and her eyes opened automatically wondering what had stopped him. What she saw made her heart race.

He looked at her with complete awe and devotion. January didn't know how to describe it, but he looked at her like she looked at her favorite pair of shoes. His eyes were soft and crinkled slightly around the edges and the corners of his mouth were just subtly tilted upward. Then January realized something. That was precisely how she was looking at Deckard. Maybe that was how she recognized his feelings; she felt the same.

Words weren't spoken as he searched her eyes. One step forward brought their bodies against each other. January's hands reached out on instinct and slipped inside his unzipped coat to rest on Deckard's hips. She wanted to feel his lips aligned with hers more than she wanted her next breath.

Deckard's kiss was one of the most addictive things January had ever experienced. She couldn't fight against the impulse to sink into him and to take everything he was willing to give. Cotton wrinkled under her fingers as she clenched her hands at the moment his full lips brushed against her mouth. He used his hands to manipulate the direction of her head, tilting her in the way he desired, and she was happy to be his puppet.

Prying her hands free from the material of his shirt, January snaked her hands up his chest until they landed on his shoulders. Expertly she slid his coat from his body, regretting that he had to remove his hands from her hair to finish the removal.

The coat fell onto the floor with a plop and Deckard broke away from the kiss as if the spell had been broken. January wanted to pull him back to her; she yearned to feel his body pressed against her again.

Her lips tingled like tiny firecrackers popped on the skin and she instinctively pressed her fingers to them. She watched in rapt attention Deckard's retreating back stalk toward her front door, flip the lock, and turn back around to stare at her.

Something shifted. The air changed and crackled between them as if a slow-burning fire was building in the space. But there was no fire, no wooden logs, no flickering flame – their chemistry is what had ignited.

A gleam in Deckard's eyes sparkled as he took her in. One foot moved in front of the other and she felt her skin pebble under his gaze. He stalked toward her, his focus never moving away from her; Deckard was a hunter tracking his prey. For every stride he made forward, January took one back. His speed started to increase, as did hers, until they were both running through her house – the hunter giving her chase.

She darted down her hallway and thought she was safe as she crossed the threshold for her bedroom, but a strong arm gripped her around the waist and held her back. Before January could catch her breath, she found herself lifted in the air and then flying across the room landing with a plop on her bed.

The bed swallowed her as her body settled, but there wasn't much time to crawl away because a heavy weight landed on top of her body.

Laughter exploded from deep in January's chest and she noticed Deckard was enjoying himself just as much. But as quickly as their hunt had started, their snickers died down. January stared up at the man that had captured her heart, his strong body towered over hers, his hips pressed against hers. January wanted nothing more than to keep their bodies aligned.

"Caught you," he murmured as he sunk down to rest on his elbows, their noses only an inch apart.

With a shaking hand, January reached up to feel the soft strands of his hair between her fingers. They felt like the finest silk. He leaned into her touch as if it were his talisman. A shuttered breath fell from his lips while her thumb gently glided back and forth across his forehead.

January loved seeing him relaxed at her touch. There was something that made her heart skip a beat at watching him so affected by her.

She felt his hand slide up her arm until it rested over hers, clasping their fingers together as he drew her arm over her head.

A magnetic force pulled their lips together and the bond was so strong that neither of them could pull apart – not that she wanted to. She felt herself slipping away into oblivion. There was no bedroom, no guilt, no loss of Christmas - it was just her and Deckard.

Their eagerness grew with each brush of their lips and swipe of their tongues. One of Deckard's hands slid down her body to rest on her waist before slipping beneath her sweater to rest on her skin. At the same time, January's leg hitched alongside his hip. A muscled thigh pressed against her center as he adjusted himself above her and she was careening into bliss.

January's hips moved on instinct, rocking against the sweet friction that his leg created. There was a tent growing in his pants as he rocked against her. January wanted to discover what he tasted like, to find out if the skin was soft, smooth, and velvety.

Her heart rate picked up when Deckard practically ripped her sweater over her head and tossed it across the room. She arched her back on impulse and he slipped his fingers along her spine to flip the hooks on her bra. He gripped the front of her lace bra, the small piece of material just between the cups, and plucked it away from her body, throwing it in the same direction as her sweater.

"Your turn," she exclaimed as she tugged at the hem of his shirt.

Deckard crawled backward off the bed and then stood at the foot of the mattress. In the way that has always amazed January, Deckard pulled at the back of his shirt and jerked the cotton over his head. His bare chest called out to her and she wanted to, needed to, touch the defined ridges. Effortlessly her upper body lifted off the bed. It felt like she had floated over to h, and bere she knew it, her fingers were tracing the dips and definitions of his abdomen.

A hiss escaped between Deckard's teeth as she knelt on the floor before him and pressed a kiss to the skin on his hip just above the waistband of his jeans. January nipped and sucked as she made her way across to the opposite side of his body.

"I want to taste you," January explained, her fingers toying with the button on his jeans, silently waiting for his permission but also not caring either way.

"Fuck," he groaned, his head falling backward as she slipped the button free, slid the zipper downward, and tugged on the sides of the denim to pull them toward the floor. His boxer briefs quickly followed.

January stared at his length for a minute. It was standing proudly with all of its impressive length and girth. She had never described a cock as beautiful before, but Deckard's easily fell into that category. Her mouth salivated in yearning.

Giving a blowjob wasn't something January did often or with a cock as imposing as Deckard's, but right now, she wanted to do nothing more. She needed to please him the same way he had pleased her.

Tentatively she wrapped her hand around the base of his shaft, not surprised when her fingers didn't come close to touching. Lightly she slid her hand up and down a few times, learning what spots were the most sensitive, then she couldn't hold back any longer.

January opened her lips as wide as possible to accommodate the erection. Her tongue tasted the pulsing vein on the underside of his cock and she followed the path until she reached the head. She couldn't take much of him inside her mouth, but Deckard didn't seem to mind as she swirled her tongue around the head.

"Holy shit," he groaned, placing his hand gently on the back of her head, sinking his fingers into her hair.

His declaration spurred her onward. She picked up her pace and her hands slid up and down his shaft as she continued to suck the head in and out of her mouth. Pressure from Deckard's hand behind her head increased her movements and she loved how he seemed to be losing control.

Then he stopped.

Deckard's chest was heaving, and as January peered up at him, he had a crazed look in his eyes. She loved that she was able to do that to him – unleash his caged animal.

"Get on the bed," he commanded. His voice was dark and menacing… It slivered around January like a viper ready to bite.

Her panties were immediately soaked.

The moment her bottom hit the mattress, Deckard lifted her under her arms and tossed her back on the bed, saying, "Taking too long." He moved so swiftly that January felt as if she was going to get whiplash as he pulled at her boots and socks. With one enormous yank, he had her jeans and panties off in one swoop of his arms, like a magician wielding his magic wand. She didn't have time to see where the clothes had landed because his mouth settled on her sex and January could barely remember her name.

He wasn't gentle or soft as he laved at her center. Deckard was almost punishing in the way he sucked and nipped at her. It was a punishment that January was all too willing to take.

But as much as she enjoyed having his mouth on her folds, she wanted to feel him inside her. She wanted that missing puzzle piece to make their connection complete.

"Deckard, please," she begged, but he ignored her, adding his thumb to circle her bundle of nerves.

Her legs started to shake on either side of his head as her pleasure rose, and before she could blink, January erupted against his mouth. So many stars twinkled in her line of sight that January was afraid she had hit her head like she had when she was younger, had fallen from a tree, and earned herself a concussion.

Deckard continued to slide his hand up and down her overly sensitive core, but his focus was on her.

"Please tell me you have protection," he pleaded. January blindly reached over and opened the drawer to her nightstand, grabbing an unused box of condoms. She carelessly tossed it in Deckard's direction. "Thank goodness."

A mewling cry broke through the silence of the bedroom when he removed his hand from her sex; it was a cry of impatience that January couldn't control.

Deckard donned the condom in record time and crawled onto the bed above her. He held his cock as he approached her entrance, rocking his hips to slide his erection up and down her slickness. It was all too much for January. She wanted to feel him inside her more than she wanted anything else in her life at that moment.

January didn't have to wait long.

She expected him to plunge himself to the hilt, take what he wanted, but he thrust in and out of her channel inch by painstaking inch. It was driving her mad, but she knew it was because he wanted her body to adjust to his size. January had never felt so full when he made it as far as he could go. And it was magnificent.

January could see that it was taking a significant amount of effort for Deckard to keep from rocking into her at a grueling rate. The vein in his neck pulsed. "Are you okay?"

"Yes," she moaned. "More."

Deckard slid his hands under her body and gripped her bottom, squeezing her flesh as he began to thrust again. January had to reach up and hold onto her headboard to keep her body from moving up the bed.

"Oh my. . ." her words trailed off as Deckard leaned forward and sucked one of her nipples into his mouth, never pausing his lunges.

Her body felt like it was on fire and the only way to extinguish the burn was to find her release.

"Turn over."

January had to pry her fingers from her headboard and then he flipped her over before she took her next breath. With his steely grip, Deckard pulled her hips into the air and plunged inside her sex once more.

January gasped at the intrusion. He was deeper this way, somehow. She had always wanted to be adventurous in the bedroom, but her poor taste in men left her always on her back when they had sex. She had a hard time asking for what she wanted. It seemed Deckard had a wide array of things up his sleeves. This new position was quickly becoming her favorite as Deckard's cock hit a spot no man had ever found before.

Her own body began to respond as it rocked back against every one of Deckard's thrusts. His hips smacked against her bottom and thighs with every push and it was one of the greatest sounds January had ever heard, trailing only behind the groans and grunts coming from Deckard.

January's core began to clinch and she knew that she was getting close to the pinnacle. It was within reach now and she could almost touch it. But then she found herself turned over onto her back again.

"I want to see your face when you come with me inside you."

January couldn't argue with him. She wanted to see his face when he came too.

This position was one January was familiar with, but she should have known that everything with Deckard would be better. He leaned over her, his arms on either side of her head, but he never slowed his movements.

January didn't take long to feel that her release was just in reach again. Instinctively her hands loosened their grip on her covers and she lifted them to touch his back, her short nails scratching at his smooth skin just below his shoulder blades.

"Yes!" she cried out as her orgasm surged through her body. Her muscles erupted in waves around his shaft that continued to drive in and out of her.

"That's it. Fuck, I'm going to come."

His already punishing pace increased, but January was too lost in her orgasm to adjust her limbs.

Deckard's body stilled above her as his hips jerked a few times, his release spilling into the condom. He curved his back to rest his sweat-soaked head on January's chest. She loved that he was seeking her for comfort after his exertion at sending them over the edge.

She scraped her fingers up and down his back and could feel each heavy intake of breath as if it were her own. Nuzzling her chest, Deckard squeezed his arms under her back and held her to him, resting his body fully against her. He was heavy with all of his muscles, but she didn't care. She wanted his comfort as much as he wanted hers.

January bent her legs on either side of his hips and cradled his large body, using one of her hands to comb through the wet strands of sweat-soaked hair on his head while the other continued to scratch his back.

His warm breath floated across her cooling skin, leaving goosebumps in its wake. "I just need another minute, and then I'll be ready."

Her motions halted immediately. "Ready for what?" She was afraid that he was referencing that he planned to leave, and that was the farthest thing from what she wanted.

Deckard propped his chin on her breastbone to look at her in confusion. "For another round. . ." He let the comment hang in the air around him.

"Oh, I thought you meant something else." Embarrassed, she flicked her hand in the air as she spoke. He captured the limb with his own and intertwined their fingers. Blue eyes searched hers, and his eyebrows raised in shock when he realized what she had been referring to.

"You thought I was going to leave?" January wasn't positive, but he sounded almost hurt by her assumption, and she hated that she was the cause.

"No! I mean, I just wasn't sure. I don't want you to leave."

He kissed her once before moving off her body and resting on his side next to her. Dropping his hold of her fingers, he reached across her waist, pressed the middle of her back, and slid her closer to him until her body molded against his.

He continued to situate her like a rag doll until her head rested on his bicep. The muscles reminded her of bulging pillows. Deckard moved her arm along his waist while his arm remained around her, trailing soft paths up and down her spine.

"This is nice," she told him after pressing a soft kiss to the middle of his chest.

"It is."

"Maybe we could stay like this a while longer? I'm sure you're tired."

Deckard didn't respond with words. He lightly rocked his hip and January could feel his rock-hard length press against her stomach.

"Oh my. Already?" she asked in surprise. She had never met a man so willing to go for another round of sex immediately after. Usually, she had to initiate hours later if she was lucky to have her lover wake up.

"You're naked and have your perfect breasts pressed up against me. Believe me, he was ready right after."

January didn't need any convincing. She was as ready to go as he was. And with a lift of her leg over his thigh, January guided him to her entrance, where he slipped inside effortlessly this time. Her body was ready for him.

This round was slow, unlike the first time, which had been rough and fueled with their desire and chemistry. Deckard took his time with her body, learning which spots gave her shivers or had her clawing at his back for more.

Deckard wasn't a selfish lover. He took his time to make sure that January was as lost in the sensations of their lovemaking as he was. His kisses were soft, but no less powerful, leaving her lips swollen from all the attention he was paying her mouth. She found her release three times before he gave into his own.

They both had to work the next day, but neither cared as he spooned against her back for the night. January typically didn't allow men to stay the night, but Deckard was different. He already held a special place in her heart and earned it in record time.

She could feel Deckard's soft breaths on her neck as he slept peacefully, but January's mind was awake with worry. She was certain now that she had fallen in love with him. She knew she had to keep three words to herself because he had plans and a life to return to in Atlanta. But that was the least of her worries.

January's mind kept asking one question.

Would he have ever loved her enough to stay if she hadn't wished Christmas away?

RENEE HARLESS

Chapter Eight

Waking up next to Deckard was something that January would never tire of. Since he slept over after the sleigh ride, it seemed just as natural for him to stay the next night as well. The transition between boyfriend and lover had always bothered January, but with Deckard, it had been seamless. Just like it seemed to be with everything involving him.

It was strange to be back at work with no celebrations looming. New Year's Day didn't draw the excitement as Christmas. The Pineville Winter Solstice Celebration had gone on without a hitch, but now there was nothing festive or cheerful to report on. She was left researching the addition of new slopes at the local ski lodge.

It all seemed wrong, especially with Christmas only two days away.

She and Deckard were going to host her family the next night for Christmas Eve dinner. It was a tradition her mother had always insisted upon, but with January's screw up, January planned to do it instead. She was thrilled Deckard offered to help even though it meant that their last night together was going to be shared with others.

"Someone is thinking about you," Samantha said as she carried in a large bouquet of Poinsettias, pulling January away from her mindless task. The red was bright and lush against the stark backdrop of her office walls.

"Hm. ..I wonder what someone would have to do to get such a lovely surprise."

January shrugged her shoulders, not wanting to share her personal business with her best friend at their office. Samantha was already aware that she and Deckard had made love on the night of the solstice celebration, but she didn't know that he had been sleeping at her house every night since then. Her best friend knew the limitations January put on her relationships.

"It is very lovely indeed," January teased as she turned back to her computer to type up her notes regarding the ski lodge. But, of course, her friend couldn't let her drop the topic as if receiving flowers was a daily occurrence. People only received gifts like this at the office when it was a birthday or someone died.

Samantha reached over and pressed the power button on January's monitor to get her attention.

"Tell me."

"There isn't anything to tell," January lied as Samantha's smile grew. Unfortunately, that meant January was going to have to spill every dirty detail.

As Samantha tapped her fingernails musically on January's desk in anticipation, she finally gave in. "Fine."

Taking a deep breath, January quickly whispered, "Deckard's stayed with me the last two nights and he's helping me host Christmas Eve dinner for my parents tomorrow." It was all said in one breath that left January slouching in her seat when she was finished.

"Wow. I'm so proud of you."

"Don't be. I think I'm crazy for pursuing something with a man I barely know and who is leaving in two days."

Samantha sat in a chair across from January's desk. The cheerful smile that had been on her lips morphed into a frown.

"So he still plans on leaving? He won't change his plans?"

"Not that he has mentioned to me. But why would he? Pineville is in the middle of nowhere."

"You're here," Samantha pointed out, but January cocked her eyebrow and shook her head.

"I knew all along that he wasn't staying. It's why I didn't want to get tied up with him in the beginning."

"Ah, so he tied you up? How was it?"

"What? No. Samantha, focus."

"Sorry. He's just so hot."

"I'm aware. Anyway, I knew better and now it's time to face reality."

"And what reality is that?"

"One where I become a lonely crazy lady that celebrates a holiday that doesn't exist and pines away for a man she had a week-long affair with."

"Well, that sure is depressing."

January leaned her head on her desk and replied, "Tell me about it."

A knock sounded on her office door and January looked up to find her boss' assistant standing with a notebook in her poised hand. She informed them that there was a staff meeting in five minutes with some changes to the current issue.

When the assistant turned away, both women groaned in unison, and January found herself slamming her head back on the desk repeatedly.

~

January wasn't sure what time to expect Deckard. They never discussed their working schedules; she just knew that he stopped by his grandparents' house to change then he would arrive at her home. Shame overcame her as she added another layer of cheese mix on top of the layer of noodles for the lasagna. January had been taking all of Deckard's time away from his family. From what she could tell, they didn't mind, but she imagined that they probably wished that he would spend at least a few hours with them.

Maybe tonight she would suggest that they spend it apart. She figured she should start getting used to the feeling of not having him around instead of filling every second and place with memories of him.

With the lasagna set up, she put it in the oven and returned to her bathroom to catch a quick shower. Her body and mind were aching after learning that they were going to cut some of the staff at work. She wasn't afraid for her own position with the Pineville Gazette. Her articles always received the most reads and accolades on the online and paper forms of the newspaper. But some of the older staff were worried that they would be forced into retirement. She only hoped that they kept Samantha on board. Her friend wasn't assigned the best items to report and she spent a lot of her time assisting with the research for January's assignments. She hated the worry that came with the wait.

The warm water felt delightful on January's sore muscles and she allowed herself a few extra minutes just to stand under the spray.

A moan echoed in the shower stall as her body started to relax. Turning around under the spray, she let the water perform the same relief on her front as it had on her back. With closed eyes and head tilted back, she let the water pound against her skin all the way up to her neck.

The squeaking of her shower door being opened caused January to twist around too fast and lose her footing. She felt herself free fall in the tiled shower stall and envisioned that this was how she would die. Another addition to those statistics of people tripping and falling to their death. Except she didn't fall. A pair of strong arms caught her around the waist and lifted her back onto her feet.

"Are you okay?" the deep voice asked as he took a step into the water spray and caressed every inch of her body while looking for a cut, scrape, or bruise – some indication that he had harmed her.

Despite being scared to death, January thought it was sweet how he was checking her over.

"I'm okay. What are you doing here, Deckard?"

He stood under the water and let it sleuth down his muscled frame. How she longed to be one of those water droplets. "I always come over after work."

"Yes, I know. But what are you doing here, in my shower?" she emphasized.

"Oh," he chuckled, his blue eyes darkening as he took in her naked form. It was like a flip was switched and alpha Deckard came out to play. "When I came into the house I heard the shower. I thought that maybe you were a dirty girl today and needed someone to make sure that you got very *very* clean."

Her shower was small, barely enough for the two of them, but it instantly felt as if it was shrinking even more in size. They were in a space with the walls closing in.

She was already turned on from watching the water cascade down his body, but his words had her sex throbbing for his touch. January captured her bottom lip between her teeth as she imagined him sliding his fingers through her folds. Her skin was covered in goosebumps from being out of the heated water, but she didn't feel chilled at all. Instead, she felt as if she was on fire.

"Do you want me to get you clean, sweetheart?" he asked as he reached out and trailed his knuckles down from the side of her neck to just below her navel. Then he paused as he waited for her answer.

January couldn't speak, couldn't tell him that she wanted to feel his hands all over her body. She nodded her head instead. The moment his hand slipped along her sex, January had to steady herself against the tiles. Her hands smacked against the cold material as two of his fingers sunk deep inside her.

A haze of lust hovered in her vision, but she could see that his dick had fully hardened. She wanted to reach out to stroke it, feel its velvety skin, and give Deckard every ounce of pleasure he was giving her. But she didn't get the chance.

"I need you now. Turn around and put your hands back on the tile." She followed his command and noticed how he had stashed a condom on the soap dish, opening the packet and protecting them both as he slid the latex over his cock.

His shaft glided into her effortlessly and she gasped at the pleasure. She tried to stay out of her head and focus on enjoying this with Deckard, but January feared she would never feel this with anyone else. The tears came quickly and she was glad the shower could wash them away. A lifetime of memories was what she was going to have to endure.

Deckard's powerful thrusts took them careening over the edge just before the shower water chilled. He quickly lathered them both with soap and washed them clean.

Her teeth chattered as she stepped out of the shower stall and grabbed her towel, tossing an extra one toward Deckard as he exited behind her. But he didn't use it to dry himself off; he took the thick terry cloth and draped it over January's shoulders, providing her extra warmth.

"I'm sorry, baby." Deckard's hands moved up and down her shoulders, trying to warm them with the friction.

"It's okay," she stuttered between her chattering teeth.

Leaning down, he lifted her in his arms and carried her into her bedroom, setting her on the bed and then moving toward her dresser.

He didn't need directions; he knew where she placed all of her things since he helped her fold clothes yesterday. Worn-in sweats were tugged up her legs and a purple long-sleeve shirt replaced the towels. He pulled her favorite fuzzy socks over her feet and looked her over, pleased with himself. She wore no panties or bra, but she dared not mention anything. He had taken the time to dress her in her favorite things to keep her warm. It was one of the nicest things anyone had ever done for her.

"Deckard," January called out as he stalked back toward the bathroom. He had almost crossed the threshold when he glanced at her over his shoulder and she added, "Thank you."

He winked and turned back around, giving January a fantastic view of his perfect ass, and though she knew she needed to check on the lasagna, she figured she could take a few extra minutes to admire perfection.

~

"This is delicious," Deckard said around a mouthful of lasagna - his second helping. "You made this?"

"Hey!" she exclaimed in jest.

As if he was being arrested, he held his hands high in the air, trying to backpedal. "No, I just meant. . ."

She erupted in laughter before explaining, "It's my mother's recipe. One of my favorites too."

"I bet it was awesome growing up with a mom who always cooked. My parents worked a lot, so we mostly ate takeout."

"My mom loved to cook. Still does. Her Christmas ham was always one of my favorites. I wish you could have had a chance to taste it. No matter how many times I try to make it, it's never quite right."

He placed his hand on hers just as she brought her fork to her mouth.

"I'm sorry I never got the chance to try your mother's Christmas feast. But I'm certain that whatever you make tomorrow will be amazing."

"You have such faith in me."

"I'm amazed by everything that you do, January." With a gentle squeeze, he released her hand and they continued eating, boxing up the leftovers for their lunch the next day.

She knew the only thing left unaccounted for on the list she had given to Deckard explaining her parent's Christmas traditions had been watching a Christmas movie. Though she rarely had the chance to see any films, watching a Christmas movie was never on her list of things to do.

But she knew a list of her family's favorites.

"I'm going to make us some hot cocoa and then maybe we can watch a movie?" she asked Deckard.

"Sounds great. I'll clean up the dinner mess."

January loved that he always did things like that. He would chip in without being asked, not only with her, but he did the same at his grandparents' shop too. He had an innate ability to know when someone needed help.

The milk was poured to fill half of the saucepan, then January set it on the stove before placing the milk jug back in the refrigerator. Next, she pulled down the chocolate powder, sugar, and vanilla to prepare the mixture.

"I'm going to queue up a movie. Can you stir the milk if I'm not back in a minute?" January asked as she turned the knob to the correct heat setting.

"Absolutely."

In a flash, she moved toward him and placed a peck on his cheek before she made her way toward her living room.

The television screen came to life as January pressed the red button on her remote. She found the option to search for movies and scrolled through the listings hoping that one of the movies she was familiar with would pop up.

She scrolled faster and faster, but none of the classic Christmas movies were available. January began to frantically type film titles into the onscreen keyboard, hoping one of them would come up.

But she was coming up empty.

"No. No, no, no!" she cried out in horror.

Deckard came rushing into the living room, looking worried.

"What's wro -" he began to ask, but January hysterically interrupted.

"It's all gone. All of them."

"What's gone, sweetheart?" Deckard placed both his hands on her shoulders and turned her to face him.

"All of the movies. I was trying to find one of the classic Christmas movies and it's like. . .they don't exist either. Not *Miracle on 34th Street*. Not *It's a Wonderful Life*. Not *The Santa Clause*. They're just. . .gone."

Her heart was racing. Her chest heaved with heavy breaths.

"Calm down, baby. You have to realize that if there's no Christmas, then they had no reason to make those movies."

January didn't know why she hadn't considered that, but the thought hadn't crossed her mind. So many people revered the movies that the idea of them not existing was something that January couldn't wrap her head around.

"But. . ." she started then her words caught on a choked sob. January didn't know why this recollection was affecting her so much.

Deckard pulled her against him and wrapped her in an embrace that soothed her instantly. His hand stroked up and down her back, and she felt like putty against his body.

"There you go. Now, were there any movies you and your family watched that may not have been Christmas movies but would mean something to you?"

A light bulb went off in January's head. Filled with glee, she pulled out of Deckard's arms and ran to her entertainment center, opening the door that encased her DVDs. She had no sorting system, so it took her a while to locate the movie, but when she spotted the particular case, January grabbed it and turned to face Deckard. Her smile was so wide that her cheeks hurt.

"*Die Hard*?"

"Yes, of course. This is one of my brother's favorites."

January didn't explain further. She popped it into her DVD player and started the film. While the movie sat in menu mode, she mixed up their hot cocoas and brought them out to the living room, resting them on the coffee table.

Deckard draped them both under a blanket as she cuddled against him on the couch.

"Ready?"

At his nod, she started the movie. She was excited to share this small thing with him, but as the movie progressed, she realized her mistake.

The movie still existed, but there was no Christmas party. The film had been altered to a simple office party and continued on as if it were meant to be that way from the start.

January was disappointed, and when Deckard looked down and saw her frown, she explained how the movie differed from what she remembered.

"I'm sorry, sweetheart."

"It's not your fault. I only have myself to blame."

January couldn't focus through the rest of the film but noticed how Deckard seemed to enjoy the classic action flick. The light from the television illuminated his face in the darkened room. She could imagine her brother, father, and Deckard lounging on her parent's large sectional couch completely lost in the movie but in a calm camaraderie. In her vision, Deckard fit in perfectly with her family.

Thumping echoed in her ears as her heart pounded. She knew without a doubt that Deckard had stolen her heart.

She realized that he was indulging her by agreeing to relieve the Christmas traditions that she used to despise, but she couldn't help but wonder if perhaps it was because he felt the same way about her.

Her eyes were drawn to the white glow of his profile; the strong jaw, straight nose, kind eyes – he was the whole package. And she felt down to her soul that he was meant to be hers, but timing stood in their way.

"Deckard," she whispered, and he pulled his attention away from the movie to gaze down at her.

"Yeah, sweetheart?"

January took a deep breath. She was about to bare herself to him in a way she had never done before. "Deckard, I -"

BANG!

A gun shootout on the screen drew their attention back to the movie and her confession was left hanging in the air. Her moment had been sidelined and she took it as a sign.

They watched the rest of the movie. Even January was intrigued by the film's plot she had never given much of a chance before.

But as they lay in bed, Deckard's chest pressed against January's body, he asked, "Hey, what were you going to say earlier?"

This was her chance to confess that she had fallen in love with him, but unlike earlier, her confidence had disappeared.

She turned over to face him and his arm automatically wrapped around her.

"Oh, it was nothing," she lied. "I was going to ask you something about tomorrow's dinner, but I can't remember anymore."

His eyes flicked back and forth as he searched hers. January worried that he would call her on her bluff and then she'd be forced to admit how she was feeling.

But she didn't want him to give up the opportunities awaiting him back home. So, she would keep her mouth shut unless she was forced to admit her feelings.

Luck was on her side as Deckard leaned forward and captured her mouth in a kiss before he settled her against him for the night. She felt his breaths even out and the rhythm of his pulse slowed when sleep overtook him. But January spent another torturous night awake, silently wishing she could fix everything.

RENEE HARLESS

Chapter Nine

At work, January tried not to think about all of the prep work that she had waiting for her at home for tonight's dinner. It wasn't just the ham she had sitting in her fridge ready to go in the oven for three hours or the handful of side dishes she had to prepare in the three hours the ham was cooking, but it was the cleaning and tidying waiting for her. January tried her best to keep a tidy home since it was just her in the two-bedroom bungalow, but she wanted to impress her siblings and their families.

They told everyone she wanted to make up for missing the solstice celebrations with him, but Deckard and her parents knew the truth. This would be the last Christmas Eve dinner she'd get to have, and she wanted to make it special.

Thank goodness she had already requested to work a half-day before the newspaper decided on cutbacks. Otherwise, January wasn't sure if she would have been able to get any of the items on her checklist completed.

The article she had been working on was drafted in the morning and sent over to the copy editor. Co-workers stopped by her office with sullen expressions, everyone afraid that they may lose their jobs in the new year, but January tried to keep focused on the night's event instead.

She had to make an unscheduled pit stop at the general store for some tablecloths to grace the buffet table she pulled out of her basement. Regret filled her for all the times she ignored the kitschy shop and opted to order online or go to the larger big box store a few towns over. January had come to love Nick's Knacks with its vast array of items and Deckard's grandparents, that always welcomed her with a warm smile.

The bell above the door chimed as she walked inside, and her eyes searched for Deckard automatically. His height and dark hair were easy to spot above the shelves. January knew he was working, and she didn't want to distract him, so she went opposite toward the housewares to grab the white tablecloth she needed. A few candles caught her attention with their red and silver swirls, and January also added those to her pile.

Stepping from the aisle, she made her way to where she had seen Deckard earlier and found him adding some flashlights to the shelves.

"Hey."

He flipped his head in her direction in surprise and smiled widely when he saw her standing there.She walked right up to him, lifted her free hand to his cheek, and kissed his bottom lip. She loved that he quickly responded to her by kissing her in return. They had a magnetism that she couldn't explain or ever wanted to.

As she pulled away, Deckard said, "Wow, this is a welcome surprise. What brings you by?"

She lifted her items a bit higher to catch his eye. "Just a few things for tonight. Stopped by on my way home."

"Well, I'll be heading your way shortly. Just finishing up a few things for my grandma."

"Okay, see you then." January lifted on her toes to press another kiss to his lips. His arm was still wrapped around her waist and he didn't loosen his hold as she tried to take a step back. "What?" she asked him.

"Everything okay?" he questioned, concern evident in his voice.

"Yeah, why wouldn't it be?"

"I don't know." Deckard paused before he freed her from his embrace, adding, "I'll be close behind you."

She waved at him as she left the aisle he was working in, tossing a farewell toward his grandparents working at the front of the store after she had her items rung up.

At home, she quickly tidied up her house after placing the ham in the oven. The small dining table was replaced with the larger buffet table, adding a mixture of chairs around the setting to accommodate everyone. January laid the covering and the placemats on the table. Using some evergreen clippings she had snipped from her own Christmas tree, she tried her best to make something festive out and situated it around the candles she had picked up at the general store. She thought it looked nice, but something was missing. It wasn't nearly festive enough.

January looked around her space, searching for a regal centerpiece to bring the design together, but nothing seemed to fit. The monogram that was a makeshift tree topper could work, but she didn't want to remove it. Shrugging her shoulders, January gave up her hunt and decided to relax before she needed to get started on the side dishes.

She remembered Deckard saying he would be over soon, but that had been over an hour ago. Needing to kill some time, January went ahead and changed into the red body-hugging dress she planned to wear for the night. The material was soft cashmere that ended just above her knees, sleeves that stopped at her elbows, and a scooped neckline. Her hair still maintained its bouncy waves from this morning, so she only needed to do a quick touch-up of her makeup.

Back in the kitchen, January poured a glass of her favorite red wine, a local merlot, and started some of the side dishes she hadn't prepared the night before. With everything almost ready to go, January took the chance to relax. Relax as much as a host could with the feelings weighing on her chest. She grabbed her phone from its dock in the kitchen and shuffled toward the living room, taking in the beautiful space that Deckard and her family had helped decorate.

With the flip of a switch, January's fireplace roared to life, and she stood back to take in its beauty. She always found the flicker of a flame beautiful. It was never constant, ever-changing its shape and color; it pushed and pulled against nature.

Flipping through a playlist on her phone, January queued up some soft music to play through the wireless speakers she had situated in the house. Standing a few feet from the fireplace, January took a large sip of her wine as she watched the flame dance to the music.

"Wow," a voice called out in wonderment.

January looked over her shoulder to find Deckard approaching her, the look of awe evident on his face. He reminded her of a child that received his most wished Christmas present.

"You are absolutely stunning, January." The compliment sank deep into her heart, knowing she'd treasure it for eternity. He leaned forward and kissed her softly, pulling back before she was done.

"Let me take off my coat and I can help you finish things. Sorry that I'm late. I got tied up."

"That's okay. I have most everything ready to go, so we have a bit of time to relax before everyone arrives."

"Well, I'll definitely take a glass of whatever you're drinking," he added as he made his way toward her coat closet to hang up his jacket.

"Sure."

January left her post in front of the fireplace and went back to the kitchen to pour a glass of wine for Deckard. Just as she placed the topper back on the bottle, Deckard walked up to her with a small bag in hand.

"This is for you." He held the bag out toward January, who traded him for the glass of wine. "Happy birthday, sweetheart." She had been peering down into the bag, but her head snapped up in surprise at the mention of her birthday.

"What? Thought I forgot?" he chuckled.

"No. I just. . .didn't expect anything. You didn't have to get me a gift."

"I know, but I wanted to." Deckard took a sip of the wine, then urged her to open the bag.

Inside the black bag with black tissue paper was a red velvet rectangle. January set the bag aside and held the container in her hand as if it were the most precious thing she had ever owned. Her eyes shot up to his again and he silently urged her to open it with a gesture of his hands.

The hinges squeaked as she popped the lid and it snapped in place. Nestled inside the box was a delicate bracelet. It was so unique. January had never seen anything like it. This was no ordinary jeweled tennis bracelet. The links were a series of intertwined snowflakes with small diamonds situated in the center. In the middle of the links was a thin, long rectangle.

January reached into the box and pulled out the bracelet, bringing it closer to her face to better look at each piece. The rectangle was engraved with her name and she recognized the script used as the same as the star Deckard had designed for her parents almost two weeks prior.

"Did you engrave this?" she asked him.

"Yeah, I did. How did you know that?" he asked in amazement.

"You engraved a star ornament for my parents. I remember the script."

"Flip it over."

Following his instruction, January flipped the bracelet in her hand and found another engraving on the opposite side of the rectangle.

"My wish," she murmured as she read the inscription. "I don't understand."

Deckard slipped the bracelet from her hold and signaled for her to hold her hand out. He began to clasp the jewelry together as he said, "If I could make any wish, it would be for you."

"Deckard," she choked out at the reality of his statement. It was the sweetest non-profession of love she had ever heard.

Once the bracelet was clasped, she launched herself at him, wrapping her arms around his neck and burying her face against the warm flesh.

"Thank you so much. It's the most beautiful present anyone has ever given me."

"You're welcome, January. You deserve beautiful things."

January wanted to tell him that because of what she had done, she didn't deserve anything, but January knew he wasn't going to listen.

Disrupting their embrace, the timer on the oven went off and January had to turn her attention back to the dinner that would be underway in a few short minutes. While she plated all the food, she instructed Deckard where she kept her matches to light the candles on the table. She only had a few minutes before her family was due and she found herself running to her bedroom to grab her heels, slipping them on her feet just as the doorbell rang.

She rushed past Deckard, who stood casually against the opening to her kitchen and then stopped short, returning to where he waited. January placed both of her hands on his cheeks and left a hot, open-mouth kiss on his lips.

"Before I forget, I want to thank you for everything. And I want you to know that you look really *really* sexy all dressed up like this." January seductively ran her eyes over his body clad in black slacks that hugged his legs and ass just right and a gray button-down shirt with the sleeves rolled up to the elbows. "Are you ready?" she tacked on as she walked backward toward the door.

"I'm ready for anything."

Taking a deep breath, January opened the door to her parents, two of her three siblings, and their significant others. June had offered to babysit for the night since they all knew January's home wasn't large enough to contain all six children running around.

She poured everyone the requested wine or beer before they all took their seats. Deckard brought everything out to the table and then took his place beside January. The holiday decorations were the first things her siblings commented on, their curiosity overwhelming. January could tell that they didn't know whether to believe her or not.

Luckily, her parents could steer the conversation away from the decor and focus on a local game show the family had been watching – everyone but January. Even now, she felt like the odd man out in her own home. Deckard must have been able to sense her change in mood because, under the table, he grasped her hand and rested it on his thigh.

"Oh, Tom," her mother cried out to January's father once Deckard offered to start clearing plates. "I left the solstice star for January in the car. Would you be a dear and go grab it?"

Dutifully her father donned his coat and went out to the car despite January assuring him that she could get it another time. She wasn't even sure what a solstice star was, and she doubted that she actually needed it.

Her back had been facing the front door, so she didn't see when her father reentered the house. The small flicker of the flame on her silver and red striped candle held her attention as her siblings chatted with her mother.

"Happy Birthday!" January jumped in her seat as everyone shouted in unison.

"What the?"

"Happy birthday, sweetie," her mother said as she reached over to hug her youngest daughter. Her father carried a small sheet cake into the kitchen with a series of candles ignited on top. On impulse, January looked over to the kitchen finding Deckard carrying small dessert plates toward the table and he winked at her as she caught his eye.

The group sang to her and then her father helped to pass out pieces of the chocolate cake to everyone. Her family had even brought presents with them. Small trinkets that January would cherish.

She didn't know if it was Deckard or her family that made this the best birthday ever. Maybe it was both, but she was going to remember this day for the rest of her life.

Her family didn't linger much longer after the cake since they all had to work the next day.

January wished that time would slow. Her time with Deckard was fleeting and she wanted to hold on just a bit longer.

January slipped off her shoes and stretched when the front door closed. This was the last Christmas Eve she would have. This day that used to always overshadow her birthday no longer existed – it was a strange thought. It was painful to consider.

In the kitchen, she found Deckard elbow-deep in sudsy water, and despite trying to get him to leave the dishes for the next day, he insisted that he clean. So she grabbed a towel and started drying the dishes as he finished cleaning them. January was just happy to be with him. It didn't matter what they were doing.

With both of them working in tandem, the task went by faster than they expected. He grabbed their wine glasses and filled them with the remainder of the merlot. Together they moved toward her living room, blowing out the candles on the dining table as she passed.

They left the lights off in the space, allowing the fire light to illuminate the room in a soft orange glow. Deckard rested on January's couch and he held his arm out for her to do the same. She sat beside him, tucked her feet up on the cushions, and cuddled against his comforting body.

The air in the room was heavy, and both of them knew what tomorrow would bring. January couldn't fight against the urge to ask if he was going to stay. Her heart would always wonder if she had tried hard enough

The glass traveled to her lips and she took a sip of the grape goodness, needing the liquid courage.

"So, there is no hope in you staying?" January knew it was direct, but she needed to know, and there was no point in asking anything else.

Sadly, Deckard shook his head. The devastation was just as evident on his face as it was on hers. "The bank approved the purchase of the practice. I'm locked in for five years at that location. I just found out today."

"Oh."

Wishes had treated her poorly in the past and January guessed that this time would be no different.

"I'm sorry, January. Is there any way you'd consider moving to Atlanta?" he asked, but he seemed to know her answer already. There was no hopeful gleam in his eyes.

"My entire family is here. Living anywhere else was not something I ever considered." And even though she and her family had rocky moments, January couldn't imagine being more than a short distance from them.

"I know, sweetheart. Do you think we could try long distance for a while?"

January wanted to say yes. She wanted to tell him that she would do whatever she could to make it work. But that wasn't a reality for them.

"As much as I want to say yes, I think we both know that it wouldn't work out. You have a demanding job, and if I get called out on an assignment, I could be gone for days or weeks."

Deckard stayed silent, but he pulled her tighter against him. There wasn't much left to discuss about their relationship. Tomorrow she was going to have to say goodbye to the man who would take her heart back to Atlanta with him.

Their glasses emptied as they watched the fire in silence, and Deckard sat the cups on her coffee table before standing from the couch. Fear leaped through her at the thought that Deckard was going to leave. Why wait until tomorrow when he could face the inevitable today?

He stalked toward the tree on the opposite side of the room and stared at the lights. The glow illuminated a small gold-wrapped gift under the tree. It hadn't been there earlier and January assumed that Deckard had placed it there when she wasn't looking. But he didn't grab the gift as he crouched beside the makeshift tree stand. He picked up a fallen ornament and placed it on the small table, then reached back down for the gold box.

"Grab the green box, too, please." She called out before he stood back up. Deckard sat back beside her with both presents in hand and put the boxes between them. "You know, you're supposed to wait until Christmas Day to open presents."

"We could start a new tradition?" he suggested, and January joined in with his soft chuckle.

"You first," January said to Deckard and he smirked at her enthusiasm.

He tore through the plain wrapping paper unveiling a generic white cardboard box. He lifted the box to find a scarf nestled inside like the one she had admired on him not too long ago, a small placard that said "Hot Doc," and a handheld engraving pen. The other two items were insignificant; it was the engraver that she spent hours scouring the internet to find that she was excited to gift him.

"Wow," he murmured as he admired the engraving kit. He took time reading the box, then set it back with the scarf and lifted the placard. "Hot doc, huh?"

"I think you're quite dreamy. I bet all the girls ask for you." He shrugged noncommittally, but the blush rose on his cheeks, giving him away.

Deckard placed the placard back in the box and grabbed the engraver again. "This is really cool. I can't wait to try it out."

"I want a picture of the first thing you engrave by hand. You'll have to text me a picture."

"Am I allowed to do that?" He asked, and against January's better judgment, she knew that she couldn't cut ties with him completely.

"Yeah. I'd like to think we can stay friends at the very least."

"I don't ever want just to be your friend, January," he murmured as he set the items back in the box, moving the package aside.

January whispered, "I don't think that we have a choice." Solemnly Deckard nodded his head.

"Your turn."

Her finger slipped under the taped fold of the wrapping and she slid the box out of the paper. Like earlier, the hinges of the larger rectangle box screeched as she flipped the lid. She was surprised to find a pair of matching snowflake earrings resting in such a large box, but then the flap of an envelope caught her eye.

"These are beautiful, Deckard." January wanted to make sure he knew how much she loved the gift. He understood the significance of the snowflake to her now more than ever.

January lifted the envelope and pulled the slip of paper from the unsealed flap. In her hand, she held a round-trip first-class ticket to Atlanta available to redeem on any date she desired. He wanted her to come to visit him.

Her eyes flew up to meet his. "Deckard. . ."

"Before you decide that Atlanta isn't for you, I would love it if you'd give me a shot to show you that we could make it work. I make a lot of money, January. We can fly back and forth whenever we want."

But it's going to hurt so much when it all comes to an end, she thought.

January didn't want to be ungrateful because she was far from it. He gave her the greatest gift of all – himself. If only she were willing to accept it. But this wasn't a fairytale. Long-distance relationships rarely ever worked out, at least the ones January knew of. They'd make it a few months, maybe a year, but they would start to tire of the travel and resent each other. She was jaded and knew it, but she couldn't turn it off.

"Just promise me that you'll try. I'm not ready to say goodbye to you yet," Deckard pleaded, and regardless of her reservations, she nodded with a watery smile.In his joy, he sealed her mouth with his, reminding her how explosive they were together with the simplest of touches.

Their tongues dueled, sliding past each other as they explored. January felt Deckard's hands land on her waist, then suddenly, she was lifted in the air and settled on his lap, but he never broke their connection.

"January," he whispered, pulling away from the kiss and resting his forehead against hers. She watched his chest rise and fall as he took heavy breaths, the buttons on his shirt almost busting loose with each intake. But then Deckard spoke and all of her attention fell back on him. "I wish that I could give you everything that you love. When I came here, I wasn't prepared to find you, and leaving tomorrow is going to be one of the hardest things I'll ever do.

"My grandma used to tell us to make a wish on the first star we found in the sky. And you don't know how many days since meeting you I wished I could give you everything that you love. Almost every day for the last ten days."

"You really did that for me?"

"Every day. You're worth every wish I could possibly have granted."

He softly kissed her again as he stood, gently placing her back on her feet. This was their last night together and the weight of that knowledge was crushing on January's breaking heart. She knew he had to leave early in the morning, far earlier than she normally woke, but he wanted to spend the night with her instead of his own family.

"Go get ready for bed. I'll be there in a minute," he suggested.

She washed her face ignoring the shade of red lining her eyes caused by holding back the tears that threatened to spill over. Her dress came off her body in a swoosh and January laid it on the chair in the corner. She considered wearing something sexy and seductive for Deckard's last night, but she remembered that he loved when she wore oversized T-shirts. At her request, she collected a few of his and donned her favorite one for the night. A blue, worn-in shirt with a baseball team logo emblazoned on the front.

He sauntered in just as she worked her way under the covers and stripped himself free of his clothes, leaving only his boxers on as he joined her in bed.

"What took you so long," she joked.

Pulling her against him, Deckard explained, "I turned off the fireplace and found the perfect spot for that ornament that had fallen."

"Dead center of the tree?"

"Of course. There was no better place."

January didn't want to break the moment, too afraid that if she spoke she would erupt in tears. But Deckard seemed to be just as pensive. He skimmed his hand down her back, slowly moving it under the hem of her shirt as the silence lengthened between them.

The moonlight slipped through her bedroom curtains, leaving a glowing strip of light across the bed. It was enough to help their eyes adjust to the room's darkness. January thought how similar her relationship with Deckard was to the light – just a tiny sliver of hope remaining.

"What can I do to make this better, sweetheart?"

January thought of a million answers: stay, turn back time, elope. Tons of crazy ideas that wouldn't work.

Instead, she said, "Make love to me, Deckard."

He eased between her legs effortlessly and made love to her until both of their bodies were well-sated and used. January watched as her small clock changed to midnight. She was afraid she wouldn't fall asleep and was too scared to lose one more second with Deckard. But as his breathing evened out, her own body began to settle against him, and her eyes closed.

Before she was fully encompassed in the darkness, January whispered, "I love you, Deckard."

And just as January succumbed to sleep, Deckard whispered in return, "I love you too."

The few days of no slumber fell on January like the weight of an elephant. She vaguely remembered saying goodbye to someone and wishing them safe travels during the night, but she was too out of it to recall much. The only other time she had felt this lethargic was when she was in seventh grade and came down with the stomach flu. January remembered not being able to move because everything hurt, including moving her eyelids to blink.

Her eyes felt like lead weights as music filled her bedroom. Usually, Deckard turned off the annoying sound, but as it continued to play, she reached across the bed to shove him awake. She pried open one of her eyes and noticed that his side of the bed hadn't looked slept in much at all. The bed was cold where he slept.

Then her dreams filtered through the back of her mind like a series of snapshots and she realized that they weren't dreams at all. She had slept through Deckard leaving.

God, did she even kiss him goodbye? She asked herself.

She tried to remember all she could from when they crawled into bed, but it was mostly small clips of him saying goodbye and kissing her fondly. The music in the background was distracting, so she reached across the bed to turn off the alarm.

But her hand paused mid-air. The chorus from "I'll be Home for Christmas" played through the speakers. Her heart paused and her breath caught. Blood began pumping through her veins at record speed.

January jumped away from the alarm clock as if it electrocuted her. She had to be imagining things. Shuffling off the bed, her feet tangled in the sheets and she fell on the floor, smacking her chin on the hard surface. The metallic taste of blood filled her mouth. She had bit the inside of her cheek as she fell. January only had the chance to wince at the pain as she scissor-kicked her legs free from the sheets.

Her house was small, the hallway narrow and short, but as she ran, January felt that the floor beneath her feet continued to grow more planks of wood - it seemed never-ending. Finally, her hands gripped the corner of the wall where the hallway met the opening to her living room.

"Oh my gosh," January murmured as she took in her space. Her hand covered her slack-jawed mouth as she looked around the room.

It was still decorated for Christmas; not much had changed, but everything had changed. In the corner sat a beautiful Christmas tree, but it was missing the bucket and handmade decorations she and Deckard had spent hours creating. Instead, a stoic classic tree her mother had placed and adorned with family ornaments took its place. Traditional white lights replaced the black and white string lights. Above the fireplace on the mantle, her mother's Christmas village lit up proudly.

Everything was as it had been. January's hand moved from her mouth to sink in her hair as the realization of it all settled. Christmas had returned. Somehow, everything was as it was before.

January worried she had been living the worst kind of dream.

The snowflake ornament that had caused the transformation hung proudly in the center of her tree – staring and mocking her. She wanted to rip it from the branch and smash it into diminutive pieces, but as she approached and held it in her fingers, January couldn't bring herself to do it. The only difference she noticed was the small brown tag missing from the ribbon.

Her shaking hand settled the ornament back in place, and she circled around her room in shock. January didn't even know what day it was. Maybe nothing had changed and she really had been dreaming, but her hope was quickly diminished as she sprinted into the kitchen. The calendar clearly read that today was Christmas by a series of Xs marking down the days.

From the corner of her eye, January caught a glimpse of a bright red color coming from her dining area. The large buffet table was still in the spot reserved for her smaller dining table, but the series of red and silver swirled candles sat where she had left them yesterday. Instead of the twigs of pine from the tree she and Deckard had chopped down, a row of fake pine garland wrapped around each of the centerpieces.

The idea that everything had changed back to how it should have been diminished as January touched the candles she had grabbed at Nick's Knacks. She didn't know what to think.

"Deckard!" she called out, hoping against all hope that maybe this meant he was still there. When there was no reply, she walked out to her living room and called out again. January knew there was little chance of him still being in her house, but nothing was as it seemed.

Dismayed, January hung her head as she shuffled back to her bedroom. What hope she may have had moments ago disappeared, and as she sat on the edge of her bed, January focused on the wood grains of the floor. She pondered what all of it meant. When she wished away Christmas, everyone had gone on living as if it had never existed, but she had remembered everything; she wondered if this was the same scenario.

The song switched on the radio and "Last Christmas" began to play. January laughed sardonically at the choice. Deckard definitely took her heart with him.

Instead of shutting off the music, January crawled back under her covers, staring up at the ceiling as her head hit the pillow. She was afraid that she had truly gone mad. Impulsively, she turned her head and looked at the spot Deckard had slept the night before, or so she thought. The pillow and crumbled sheets looked as if someone had been there, but January couldn't be sure. There was only a slight indentation where a body would have laid.

The tears began to build and spill over before she could stop them. As if her heartbreaking last night wasn't enough, she had to relive it again today. Her body curled into itself as she reached over to cradle the pillow where Deckard had rested his head against her chest.

Minutes passed as January cried over the loss of her love and the time she couldn't get back with him. These were soul-crushing sobs that left January exhausted and her eyes drifted closed as her mind lulled her back to sleep.

Darkness soothed her in a way nothing else could.

A ringing noise woke January with a start, and she tried to blink, but her crusty lids were sealed shut. The pitfalls of falling asleep while crying. She rubbed her eyes with the back of her hand and then reached out to grab the phone, pressing the answer button without looking.

"Hello," her scratchy voice greeted.

"Where are you, sweet pea?" her father asked.

In confusion, January asked, "What?"

"It's Christmas. We're all waiting on you."

"Oh!" she sat up in bed with panic. "I'm sorry, I just. . ." she said, then she remembered what she had woken up to an hour ago - the loss of Deckard.

Somehow her father seemed to understand and he soothingly said, "Just get here when you can. Though I'm not sure how long the little ones will wait."

"I'll be there soon. I'm sorry," she tried to stifle down another sob, but the tremors escaped her voice.

"Hey, it's okay, sweet pea. We'll wait for you. And we all want you to know that we enjoyed dinner last night. It was a nice change of pace."

The confirmation that she had hosted dinner last night gave her a little peace of mind.

They ended the call and January clicked the music off her alarm, noting that she had fallen back asleep for about thirty minutes before her father had called. Forcibly, January had to pull her body away from Deckard's pillow that she still held against her body.

In the corner of the room sat the red dress she had worn last night and she remembered the look Deckard had given her when he saw her standing by the fireplace. No man had ever looked at her like that. She wished she had taken a picture of it as a keepsake.

"No more wishes," January scolded herself as she scooted off the bed.

Rushing through a shower, January tried not to remember how Deckard had taken her in the small compartment a couple of days ago. She pulled on a blue sweater and her favorite pair of denim, adding her trusty knee-high brown boots to complete her outfit.

She did her makeup and tried to cover up the dark circles and puffiness around her eyes, resulting from hours of crying, but there was only so much that the concealer could accomplish. Quickly, she dried and curled her hair into soft waves and took one final glance at her appearance in her full-length mirror.

Something was missing, but January couldn't put her finger on it. Then she remembered the gifts Deckard had given her or hoped he had given her.

An antique silver jewelry box sat on her dresser, and when January opened the lid, she found the snowflake earrings and bracelet nestled inside. She breathed a heavy sigh of relief that they were where she remembered placing them. January feared that Deckard was just a figment of her imagination if they were missing. And right now, her mind wasn't something that she could completely trust.

The earrings sparkled against the lobes of her ears as they caught the sunlight peeking through the curtains of her bedroom. With a gentle hand, she took out the bracelet and brought it close to her face to reread the inscription. It hadn't changed, and that was the first thing that gave January a reason to smile.

It took a few attempts to get the clasp to close, and January never understood why bracelets had to be so difficult for one person to attach.

Now when she looked back in the mirror, she felt put together. The jewelry had been the missing piece. It made her feel as if Deckard was still with her, even though he was probably already back in Atlanta.

Grabbing her phone, January pulled up his number and pressed the call button. She didn't know what she would say to him, but she wanted to hear his voice. But as the phone rang repeatedly and no one answered, she felt dejected. He was the calm in the hurricane of her life. Instead of leaving a voicemail, January shot off a text message wishing him a Merry Christmas and saying that she hoped he had a pleasant flight. Hopefully, he'd call her later and she would hold onto that sliver of hope with both hands.

As she was leaving, the photo in the hallway by her front door caught her eye. The same one Deckard had stared at the first time he had been at her house. It had seemed so long ago that he had barged into her life, but it had only been two weeks. She tried to see what he did when he looked at her family. He saw beyond her fake smile the sad woman who felt like an outsider. He saw her.

She longed to go back and make things right with herself and her family. Time and happiness were lost due to her petulance.

But maybe she could use this chance to make everything right.

~

The drive to her parent's house was quick since there were very few people on the roads. Her father opened their front door to her and hugged her tightly before unleashing her toward her nieces and nephews.

Everyone had gathered around the large dining table as they waited for her to arrive, drinking coffee and snacking on the brunch her mother had prepared. January apologized for being late, but the group sent sad looks in her direction.

They knew.

They all knew her heart was breaking and she was here only to make appearances. But they didn't realize how much she yearned to be here with them. She had a turning point as she left her house and come hell or high water, January was going to make sure that her shattered heart wasn't going to ruin their Christmas.

She smiled and waved at the group, doing her best to make it as sincere as possible, and the group collectively smiled in return, their shoulders relaxing in relief.

January moved into the kitchen and found her mother standing at the stove, stirring something in a pot. She walked up behind her and wrapped her arms around her mother's waist, hugging her in a way that silently professed her apologies for all the years she had put a damper on her mother's holiday celebrations.

"Merry Christmas, sweetie," her mother murmured as she twisted around and kissed January's head.

"Merry Christmas, Mom."

With her niece's insistence, January made a batch of hot cocoa despite April's mock devilish glare the girl's mother was sending her way. She left the adults to talk in the kitchen as she went into the large den to see some toys the kids received from Santa, but she knew they were all excited to open the presents from her parents.

It took a few more minutes for everyone else to trickle into the den and the kid's excitement grew ten-fold. The adults took their seats on the couch and single chairs. Everyone was paired together. Even her mother sat on the arm of her father's chair as they watched Augustus hand the kids their gifts.

January took a few steps backward toward the corner of the room and slid down the wall to sit on the floor. There weren't any more open seats and no one moved to make a spot for her. Moments like this made her feel like an outsider in her family, but maybe she had been looking at it all wrong. She had always isolated herself from everyone making little attempt to join them. They knew about her disdain for the holiday, so they never asked her to join them.

Augustus was crouched under the tree, reading out the names on each label as he passed the gifts out. He startled and almost knocked the tree over when January grabbed the present in his hand.

She noticed that the room had grown quiet as she had deserted her spot against the wall and moved toward the tree.

"Can I help?" she asked her brother. He blinked at her with a blank gaze then his smile grew as he let January take the present in his hand.

It was a family tradition to allow the youngest child to go first, and January held her youngest niece in her lap as she helped the toddler tear into the wrapping paper.

It was the most fun January had had on Christmas since she could remember.

An hour later, the carpet was covered in hundreds of pieces of multicolored wrapping paper as the kids played with their new treasures. She particularly enjoyed helping her eldest niece put on the makeup that January had gifted her. The cross expression on her brother-in-law's face was easy to ignore as she applied another layer of lipstick on the almost-teenager.

"Do I look as pretty as you?" her niece asked.

"You're beautiful without makeup," January told her, noticing her brother-in-law's sigh of relief at her response.

The doorbell rang and her mother went to answer the door for another one of their many neighbors that stopped by on Christmas Day. They had already had three couples drop off plates of goodies since January arrived.

She was busy explaining to her niece the use of each makeup brush and how to handle them so that she didn't see her mother reenter the room.

"January, you have a guest," her mother called out as she stood next to January's father's vacated chair.

She looked up in surprise and almost dropped the brush she was holding. "Deckard?" she asked as she stood up.

Sheepishly he shrugged his shoulders, but his gaze never strayed from her. "Merry Christmas."

On autopilot, January replied, "Merry Christmas."

He pulled his stare away and looked at the room filled with her family, which had all grown quiet as they took turns looking between both of them. "Can we. . .uh. . .talk? Privately."

"Yeah, sure." January handed the makeup brush back to her niece and nervously wiped her hands on her jeans. Her steps felt as if blocks of concrete weighed them down. Each tread took longer than the previous.

"Mom, can we use the sunroom?" she asked her mother, but she never pulled her eyes away from Deckard, afraid he would vanish into thin air.

"Sure, sweetie."

He followed her down the hallway and through the kitchen, which had a door leading to the sunroom. It was decorated from top to bottom in Christmas décor. A room that January refused to step foot in during the holidays now made her smile as she stepped inside.

In the middle of the room, January turned around and looked at Deckard, wondering what he was still doing in Pineville with a stare of awe and adoration in his eyes as he drank her in.

"Deckard, what are you doing here? Why aren't you in Atlanta?" she questioned.

"I remember, January. I remember everything."

She furrowed her brows in bewilderment. "I don't un -" she began, but Deckard placed his hand on the back of her head and kissed her.

"Last night, I wished you could have everything you loved. The ornament was the snowflake you had told me about."

Her eyes widened in shock as she recited the poem that had been attached to the ornament when she received it. "Make a wish, say it twice."

"I remember everything, just like you had with Christmas."

"You helped me realize that I actually loved Christmas all along, and it came back," she whispered in surprise. "But why are you here?"

He smiled down at her indulgently. "Because I love you, January."

Automatically she replied, "I love you too." Then he paused, waiting for the revelation to come to her. "Oh! I love you! You're here because I love you," she said bouncing on her toes enthusiastically.

"I'm guessing that's how it works."

"So does that mean you're staying? What about the loan and your practice?"

He held up the gold bag between them for her to take. January gripped the string handle and pulled out the folder tucked between the tissue paper. She flipped over the pages and then looked up at Deckard, silently begging him to explain as she placed the folder of loan papers back into the bag

"It seems as if the loan I had been approved for is here in Pineville, for a practice of my own. The tickets for my flight were canceled, and the large practice I was working at in Atlanta had already brought on a new partner.

"Believe me, I have no idea how any of this works, but I woke up at my grandparents this morning and remembered everything from last week. Cutting down the Christmas tree, making our own ornaments, the sleigh ride, and how much I love you."

He was staying, for her. He loved her enough to give her everything she desired.

"This is. . .the best Christmas ever."

"I don't know. I'm hoping that I can top this one day," he explained as he drew her into his arms. Deckard's lips met hers and she melted against him, wrapping her arms around his neck.

"How are you going to do that?" she asked, brushing her lips against his.

"You'll have to wait and see."

"Hm. . ."

"January." The words were a whisper against her mouth and she pulled away to look up at the man she loved with all of her heart.

"Are you ready to start a new tradition?"

It didn't take her long to ponder his question. She nodded as she said, "Yeah. Yeah, I am. Merry Christmas, Deckard."

"Merry Christmas, sweetheart."

Epilogue

January placed the tote on the floor and then gazed back at the freshly cut tree she had arranged in the corner of her home. Her mother had chosen the same spot the year before.

She wondered if this excitement flooding through her veins was what everyone else had felt when Christmas approached. It had been one year since she had experienced the fear that she had wished away everyone's favorite holiday. The guilt had been suffocating, but everything had righted itself.

Stepping over to the tote, she reached inside and grabbed the string lights knotted inside. It took an entire half an hour to unwind the mess. January wondered the whole time how something she neatly stored the year before had become such a mess but assumed it was one of the many unanswered questions of the world.

Using a dining chair to stand on, January started draping the lights around the tree, beginning at the top and working her way down. It was harder working on her own, but she felt accomplished when she was finished.

The rest of the box contained the garland for her mantle and the Christmas village her mother gifted to her. She made quick work of setting up the figurines and swathing the mantle in the lushness of the pine.

It was only a few days until Christmas and January knew that she was decorating much later than most. But her new traditions were hers to start.

Flicking the switch for the lights, she found her smile growing as the twinkles sparkled against the branches. The sound of the front door opening drew her attention over her shoulder. Deckard walked into the living room carrying a brown cardboard box.

"Sorry, Grandma wanted to chat when I picked up the ornaments," he explained as he crossed over to where she stood, dropping the box on the couch.

"That's okay." She smiled at him as he drew her close for a kiss. "Ready for two weeks of vacation?"

"You have no idea," he whispered against her mouth.

They had grown in spades since he moved his practice to Pineville. The transition hadn't been as seamless as they had hoped. He had to sell his home in Atlanta and then help to transition his patients to new dentists. He didn't officially move in with her for three months.

His practice flourished in Pineville and January couldn't be happier for him.

"You got started without me," he pouted as he took in the tree.

"Just the lights. They were a tangled mess."

"Fine. That means I get to hang the first ornament."

Deckard's hand slid down to hers, intertwining their fingers together. His thumb flicked the three-carat ring he had placed on her finger over the summer.

"I love you," she said, looking up at him with all the adoration she felt.

He looked down at her with the smirk she adored so much. "I love you too, sweetheart."

Together they opened up the box of ornaments Deckard had brought with him as well as the ones January had saved from last year. Christmas music filtered through the speakers as they sang along to the classic tunes.

There was one ornament left – the one that changed everything. January hesitated as it dangled from her fingers. The note she initially found with it was long gone despite the hours she and Deckard had spent searching for it the year before. January could barely recollect the saying herself. But the thought that this silly piece of glass held a particular form of magic still frightened her.

"What's wrong, babe?" he asked her from behind the tree. Her lack of singing must have alerted him.

"I'm almost afraid to hang it."

Deckard came from around the tree, and when he saw the ornament she was holding, he gave her a knowing nod.

"It deserves to hang on the tree. After all, it brought me you."

She pondered for a moment before delicately placing the glass snowflake high up in the center of the tree.

"There, now it's perfect," Deckard claimed as he wrapped an arm around her waist. January did the same, resting her head against his chest.

They stood together admiring their work before he pressed a kiss to the top of her head. "Are you ready for tomorrow?"

"Of course. Are you?"

"You know that I am. We have that dinner tonight. We should probably go get ready."

"Probably," she repeated as she turned and leaned against Deckard. "Should I wear the red or blue dress?"

"The red. Definitely red."

"A favorite of yours?"

"If it's the red dress you wore on Christmas Eve last year, it is definitely a favorite. And the star of many of my fantasies."

She giggled and then asked, "Am I at least starring in these fantasies?"

He gave her a smirk that silently answered for him before he reached down and lifted her onto his shoulder, carrying January fireman-style

"I think we have enough time that we can live out one of my fantasies right now."

And to January, that option didn't seem like a bad idea, especially when they forgot about the red dress as he dropped her on the bed.

They lost track of time as Deckard took pleasure in worshipping her body, arriving at the dinner an hour late.

~

It was colder than January expected, but the light snow fell around her, and she was lost in its beauty. Red and silver ribbons lined the pathway all swirled together. As the sleigh trudged through the snow, she pulled her ivory blanket tighter.

They were nearing the clearing where she and Deckard had watched the stars, and it was one of their favorite spots to come all year long.

"Almost there."

"Yep," she replied, adrenaline starting to swirl through her body, instantly warming her.

"I love you, sweet pea."

January turned her attention away from the swirling ribbon and looked at her dad with his pink cheeks from the bite of the cold.

"I love you too, Dad."

The sleigh stopped just outside the clearing and a group of people rushed forward to assist January in getting out of the sled. It was hard with the layers of delicate lace adorning her wedding dress.

Her father quickly joined her, and as she slipped her hand around his arm, he patted her hand.

"Cold?" he asked now that she had left her blanket and coat in the sleigh, but January shook her head. Her excitement was all the heat she needed. It also helped that the farm rented small heaters to keep the guests warm as they waited.

When Deckard had proposed at this same spot over the summer during a midnight picnic they had taken, they both knew this was where they wanted to say their vows. They also agreed unanimously on the date without a second thought. Her sister didn't even mind sharing her anniversary date. The winter solstice was the perfect day for them.

And though it was a weekday, many of their friends and family made it out for the occasion – even Deckard's family from Atlanta were decked out in their elegant wear for the event.

The farm was allowing them to rent the back part of the barn for the reception and she couldn't wait to see what Samantha had come up with. Her best friend had been one of many laid off from the newspaper, but she had a knack for planning events. Her friend opened her own business and hadn't looked back.

One of Samantha's crew handed her a bouquet of red Poinsettias as her best friend approached wearing her burgundy maid of honor gown. She carried a small bouquet of the same flower but in white.

Samantha kissed her cheek, then nodded for the music to begin, and she made her way toward the makeshift aisle.

They were masked by a gathering of trees and bushes, keeping them from being visible to the guests.

January was next and she bounced on her toes, ready to get to Deckard. She bet he looked so handsome in the tuxedo. And as she made her entrance toward the aisle, she could just make out Deckard over the bushes. January wasn't disappointed.

Deckard stood proudly under the garland-wrapped wooden arch with the officiant. The black tuxedo fit his body like a glove and she wondered if they could get an extension on the rental because she had a lot of fantasies of her own she wanted to try out that involved that suit.

Her father paused before they turned the corner, and when the music changed, they turned the corner. The aisle was long, but it was close enough that she could see Deckard's mouth drop and murmur, "Holy shit," as he got his first glimpse of her. Her father must have noticed as well because he chuckled beside her.

At the end of the aisle, her father placed January's hand into Deckard's and kissed her gently on the cheek before taking his seat next to her mother.

"You look, wow," Deckard whispered as they moved under the arch. "This may beat the red dress."

January laughed as they turned to face each other. "You look handsome, doctor. I have ideas for that tux."

The officiant in front of them coughed and they both turned toward him and quietly apologized.

"Ready?" he asked them both as Deckard squeezed her hand.

In unison, they replied, "Very."

~

January spun around the wood slate floor with her hand held tightly by Deckard's. Since they arrived at the reception, they hadn't left each other's side.

They were both amazed at the barn's transformation by Samantha's handiwork. It was a rustic dream of lace and lights. And perfect for them.

"Are you having a good time, Mrs. Spruce?" Deckard asked as he spun her back into his arms.

"I am. How about you, husband of mine?"

He tilted her back in a low dip, then kissed her thoroughly. Her hand came up to rest on his cheek during the kiss, and as he raised her back onto her feet, she left her hand in its place. She loved the feel of his skin under her palm.

"I'm the happiest I've ever been," he replied.

If it was possible for her body to glow in happiness, she imagined it would light up the entire space.

The music changed to a slower song and Deckard wrapped one arm around her waist using his opposite hand to gather hers from his cheek. He settled their clasped hands against his chest. They swayed back and forth, kissing when they couldn't hold back.

"Do you think we'd be here if you hadn't made that wish on the snowflake?" he asked her as they moved close to where their parents danced.

January didn't need time to contemplate. She already knew her answer.

The swaying stopped as she leaned on her toes to kiss Deckard again on his lips – something she would never tire of.

"I think we were meant to be together, regardless of the wish. Everything happened as it should and I beleive we would have fallen in love and found a way to be together regardless. It would have been hard, but we would have found a way. You were meant to be mine, Deckard."

"Yes, I was. But I do have one more wish."

"Really? What's that?" January was worried. She had assumed everything was perfect for them and that there was nothing that he would change.

"That you know you will always be my wish."

Tears threatened to form and January did the best she could to blink them away – she had cried enough today.

She tried to smile. It wobbled, but she grinned nonetheless. He had made the best kind of wish. It was the same one that he had made a year ago.

"You'll always be my wish too, Deckard. Always."

The End

If you enjoyed this book sign up for reminder's of Renee's future works.

www.reneeharless.com/newsletter

RENEE HARLESS

Stay in Touch

Newsletter: http://bit.ly/2WokAjS

Author Page: www.facebook.com/authorreneeharless

Reader Group: http://bit.ly/31AGa3B

Instagram: www.instagram.com/renee_harless

Bookbub: www.bookbub.com/authors/renee-harless

Goodreads: http://bit.ly/2TDagOn

Amazon: http://bit.ly/2WsHhPq

Website: www.reneeharless.com

RENEE HARLESS

Acknowledgments

This one is for all of the readers and friends that have stuck by me through the years. I wouldn't have been able to take this journey if it wasn't for you all.

To my family, your love and support means everything. I love you all so much.

RENEE HARLESS

About the Author

Renee Harless is a romance writer with an affinity for wine and a passion for telling a good story.

Renee Harless, her husband, and children live in Blue Ridge Mountains of Virginia. She studied Communication, specifically Public Relations, at Radford University.

Growing up, Renee always found a way to pursue her creativity. It began by watching endless runs of White Christmas- yes even in the summer – and learning every word and dance from the movie. She could still sing "Sister Sister" if requested. In high school, she joined the show choir and a community theatre group, The Troubadours. After marrying the man of her dreams and moving from her hometown she sought out a different artistic outlet – writing.

To say that Renee is a romance addict would be an understatement. When she isn't chasing her kids around the house, working her day job, or writing, she jumps head first into a romance novel.

www.ingramcontent.com/pod-product-compliance
Lightning Source LLC
Chambersburg PA
CBHW021138110726
47900CB00002B/407